W9-ADX-547

Is This What
Other Women Feel Too?

Also by June Akers Seese

JUNE AKERS SEESE

Is This What Other Women Feel Too?

Dalkey Archive Press

Library of Congress Cataloging-in-Publication Data
Seese, June Akers, 1935-
  Is this what other women feel too? / by June Akers Seese.
  I. Title.
PS3569.E356I8   1991   813'.54—dc20   91-3476
ISBN 0-916583-82-1

First Edition, October 1991
  second printing, December 1991

Partially funded by grants from The National Endowment for the
Arts and The Illinois Arts Council.

Dalkey Archive Press
1817 North 79th Avenue
Elmwood Park, IL 60635

*Printed on permanent/durable acid-free paper and bound in the
United States of America.*

Acknowledgments

For Debra Macut, the actress, who quit her job and came to North Carolina to play the lead in "Near Occasions of Sin." For Debra Macut, the actress, who has style and character and a following.

For Pearl Cleage, the teacher, who noticed how often what we—she and I specifically—write has to do with trying to understand the mysteriousness of sex.

For John O'Brien and Paul Evans, the editors, who knew what to cut and when to stop.

For Carolyn Phelps, the lifelong friend.

PART ONE
The Book Business

◢ 1

We all wore bras in 1954. Detroit was waiting for a recession. McCarthyism had cleared out Wayne University's famous names and scared the rest. The FBI watched the Young Socialists Club, from a distance. Sororities were a joke; and the football team played to a crowd of fifty somewhere downtown. Woodward Avenue divided the campus from the ghetto where cops walked in pairs and carried nightsticks. Most students had fathers who carried black lunch pails and talked of starting their own businesses. Fathers who were afraid of recessions and seated on McCarthy's side of the fence. Union men in a city of immigrants who refused to learn their places.

Hemingway was the big gun in the English Department, but *Lady Chatterley* was passed around. We knew little about the British upper classes, but we wrote without recourse to adjectives and yearned for our very own gamekeeper.

My first lover wore workboots and affected a Slavic accent. He had staked out Walter Reuther's 1933 itinerary through Europe and followed in his footsteps. He was a transfer student from Swarthmore, but I found that out later. I thought I'd found the Lawrentian ideal in a Pendleton wool shirt until the afternoon he invited me home to Palmer Woods where his maid baked cherry pies on the cook's day off. I kissed him good-bye fast. I hate liars.

There were standard phrases that year. New to me, but standard: "She has a lot of miles on her." What might have been a car or a railroad train was my friend of twenty-eight who seemed sophisticated, who walked a little stooped against the snowy blasts of January air in her fitted, hooded coat. Who amazed her English professors with her tight prose style and wordless presence in their night classes.

My new lover was the one with the standard language. He wore wingtip shoes and a tweed hat with a feather and took night trains to New York City. I thought he was sophisticated, too; but his words made me pull back. We were sitting on a board in my apartment talking about the book business and Russian counts, and how many times the third name had changed in Farrar, Straus and Cudahy.

It's Giroux now; and the publishing business may have settled down some. I have. Then, I wanted to keep on listening and asking, but I was stuck in that phrase. "Is this what men say about unmarried women who do not sleep alone?" I turned away.

It seemed like a cruel remark, and it frightened me. The image of my friend Parker stuffing Kleenex in her bra in the dim light of my bathroom made me feel that her prose style and ambition wouldn't help much. My new lover knew all about her brains; he had introduced her to his friends at Scribner's and written letters to editors who were away at the beach. August is a steamy month in the city.

When Parker finally moved to Manhattan, she wrote me long letters about the thin trees on Park Avenue and the antique shops on Third. None of her letters has yellowed in twenty years.

Sept. 25, 1955

Dear Katie:
Read a review of *Miss Lonelyhearts*, which stopped me dead. About how it's hard to laugh at the need for beauty and romance, no matter how tasteless, even disgusting, the results are; and there is nothing sadder than the truly monstrous. Made me think of so many kinds of people I've always felt a sort of affection for, without knowing why; and West got it! Like young hoods with their pretty haircuts and shocking pink shirts; and flamboyantly dressed girls, I mean poor ones, with those hideous products of Woolworth's; and people who flock to Times Square to see jungle movies to get a kick.
Love,
Parker

In the afternoons, the September she left, I muddled along renting out reproductions and typing their history on blue file cards at the Detroit Institute of Arts. My boss was an anti-Semite who removed part of the brochure if the person on his mailing list had what he called a "Jewish name." I sat in the locked bathroom stuffing the missing parts back after he left for the day. The museum guard was a policeman with two degrees—tall and good looking, a family man. We drank coffee together and decided we both had cushy jobs. Sometimes a man crated paintings in an adjoining room, and you could hear his staple gun. When I left the building, the street lights were on, and the guard walked me to the door.

I ate supper alone in a cheap restaurant next to the Maccabbees Building. Soupy Sales and his entourage would be sitting in the coffee shop as I passed: mindless, manic, a man with a crazy style. I entered the restaurant, passed the Ukranian cashier who talked to herself, and ordered a fruit salad. The ceiling fans turned, and I picked out the slimy peaches and tried to cool off.

My apartment had a Murphy bed, a dressing room, and no furniture. It also had a galley kitchen with doors. A trumpet player lived upstairs, next door to a mother-and-son team who drank themselves into a fury every night and pleaded with each other to "let up." I read in bed with the radio off. I wrote on legal pads, and my pencils came from work—already sharpened.

My lover with the ready-made judgments was married. I didn't know it until Christmas. I never thought to ask. His hours were not his own. They weren't mine either. I had a lot of time to think, and my mind wandered. Without a husband to protect you from the words of other men, everything is harder. Not much room for talk or sex; and though I have never had to stuff Kleenex in my bra, it was not a lush life.

Mornings were more dependable. I crammed history classes, back to back, and took a fencing course for lunch. I had failed swimming and wanted a sure thing. Nineteen-fifty-five became 1956, and I fell asleep before Lawrence Welk even got started.

There was a blizzard that winter. Sensible people stuck their snow shovels in the drifts and walked indoors and opened a bottle of brandy. It's always a drag after Christmas. Everything is due, and the air is too cold to breathe.

My head was packed with names of English kings and speeches on Irish Home Rule. Two of Parker's letters arrived that morning. I juggled things around and stayed home. I made a deal with the paperboy to bring back a sack of potatoes when his route was over. Then I crawled back in bed and opened the first letter.

I skipped over the part about her job:

Jan. 3, 1956

Dear Katie,

. . . went to a real 'hipster' party in the Village, with a creep. Bongo drums, police raid, etc., all followers of Kerouac and his brand of juvenile delinquency. . . . San Francisco school of Beats . . . based on kicks, kicks, kicks, Man; and all pretty empty. They affect black leather jackets, affect a love for jazz, and all smoke tea, of course! Let me hear from you, and make it good and lively.

Love,
Parker

The second letter was written during a hangover. She, too, had a day off; and the landlady was in and out; and her memory suffered as much as her head. Her handwriting scratched its way through a bad joke and ended when her pen ran out of ink. I dozed off—the kind of sweaty sleep that killed Sunday afternoons at home when I still had the illusion of escape.

When I woke up, the windowsill had little drifts, and there was a knock at the door. Standing next to my sack of potatoes and neat pile of change was my pal with the conventional life who pretended otherwise. I stopped using the word *lover;* it described nothing and sounded leftover from the twenties. He brought a stack of paperbacks tied with kitchen string and smiled at me. His eyebrows were gray from the snow. I was wearing slipper socks and a flannel nightgown. "The buses aren't running," he said, lighting a cigarette off the stove. Though crammed with deadlines, my life felt like gray slate; and I was afraid to settle into this tryst—this time-out that would have been all I wanted, two months earlier.

I pushed the bed up. The potatoes had already made a little pile of dust on the floor. We walked to the board and sat down. I planned to build my own sofa and came to my senses in the middle of a sneezing attack while hunting for old pillows in a junk shop.

"You know, Francis, I'm thinking of becoming a nun; it's not too different from what I have now. Better clothes and a more specialized reading list; and I can kiss this Murphy bed good-bye!"

"Some things aren't funny," he said, looking at my nightgown. It hid everything, and the sleeves were too long.

I have a brittle laugh that's worse when I cry, and I couldn't stop. That's all. I asked him to leave, and he did. I fell asleep. My dreams were filled with his narrow chest and five o'clock shadow. I got a powerful quote from Yeats on his personal stationery a few days later with a long comment on my mind. After that, I wore looser dresses and found out more about men from the guard at the museum than from any novel: "Meat and potatoes on the table and you in bed," he told me.

I still live in Detroit, and I have always been a good listener. The other day I heard a man on the bus make a filthy remark about the size of Gloria Steinem's crotch, and I was reminded of my friend with the New York job and all the miles that have passed and phrases you no longer hear anybody use.

It's a hot, sticky night, and somebody's TV in my building cuts from channel to channel, endlessly. I feel as lonely now as my friend with the flat chest must have felt then; sweating in a double bed with a throbbing forehead and wet underwear. I live with an Irishman who can leave my naked body and all the moaning that goes with it and go straight to the kitchen and tell me what a hopeless woman I am, while slamming cupboard doors and throwing out leftovers from the refrigerator. It's so abrupt that the suddenness of it anesthetizes me, and I feel too drained from the sex to react to the attack.

I'll never understand men, their timing, what they expect, their words. It's worse living alone. Crying doesn't help. Neither does cleaning the kitchen. I waxed the cupboard doors yesterday, but my mind never lingers on mayonnaise and roasting pans. It doesn't linger on sex, either. I used to think it was something more than scratching a scab or eating prime rib.

◢2

The First Summer

Dear Katie,

I hadn't been here long enough, just settled in my job at Random House and about to sign a lease on an apartment, when who shows up but Francis, rattling on about the book business and how unmercifully hot it is in Detroit. Francis never gets to the point until the ice is melting in the Cutty Sark and I'm deciding whether I can do without dinner if we shift the scene Uptown and eat a few more peanuts.

We ended up at that little bar next to the Cherry Lane Theatre trading stories with the bartender who claims he has been both Sylvia Sidney's and Fanny Hurst's lover. Finally, the bartender closed up and continued grandstanding a girl from NYU who was impressed with the image of Truman Capote stretched out on the back cover of *Other Voices, Other Rooms* in that famous love seat. The bartender had a few stories about Truman and his shoestring ties—and a few more about the middle-aged woman who has been Capote's secretary for years. The woman turned out to be Truman who sounds exactly like a middle-aged woman!

There's no getting around it. In New York, it's feast or famine. Three plays in a weekend or flat broke. Francis for the duration or rain and nobody to talk to but the waiters at the Blue Angel. Overtime and manuscripts to read at home, or the whole empty month of August with the authors and agents at the Cape seeing if they can spot their analysts on the sand.

At night when I'm alone I think about money. I think about you. I think about Francis. Would it be any different if we had trust funds? Three girls in editorial do. For Christ's sake, write me a letter.

Parker

The letters kept coming. Parker swears she doesn't mail them on the same day, but they come in pairs. That's fine.

My boss gets on my nerves, but most of working is keeping your mouth shut and swallowing crap, anyway. He came from a small town in the Upper Peninsula, and his mind is even smaller. Mr. Fleishmann walked through the office today; he's new on the board. My boss could hardly wait for him to get out of reach before he listed every stereotype in Sociology 101, in running order, and then waited for my response. "Mr. Fleishmann should go on a diet," I tried to throw him off. He glared at me and slammed the typewriter carriage with a force that made the secretary jump in her seat. She offered to type the report for him, and that made him even madder.

I tried to save the letters for supper, but my curiosity got the best of me, and I read one in the toilet. Parker gave me her best foot forward:

March 18, 1956

Dear Katie,
I feel conscience-bound to point out to you that the pace here is 50 times more frantic than Detroit, and you'll be more alone than you've ever been in your life. Even knowing one person, as I got to know, say Maggie, is not enough. You don't realize how much you depend on a so-called circle of people. I've written you all the highlights, but there have been many, many gray stretches which aren't worth putting in a letter. I happen to love publishing, but, most of all, New York; however, if this were all, this being my present situation socially, I wouldn't stay here. I expect things to get better.
Let me know what you think of this graybeard stuff. We've

got tickets to see *My Fair Lady* and my purse is groaning
mightily. Good thing I like to spend money!
Love,
Parker

I was thinking of moving there when I graduate. Two years
away. What's the point of such a monologue? I'll have to think
about it, and her.

I feel like squeezing a tree limb until spring pops out of it. You
can smell spring in the air. A tease. Now that Francis is out of the
picture, I have perfect concentration. I stare across the courtyard for hours. An engineering student from Israel moved in
with his girlfriend, and they cook food that smells wonderful and
then pull the shade. You don't have to live in New York to feel
friendless. What circle of people? The museum guard and my
landlady? She's senile, and if I see one more roach crawl under
the door, I'll scream.

I read the second letter in bed. It cheered me up some:

April 4, 1956

Dear Katie,
New York has been fabulous this past week, with green sprouting
out everywhere and people wearing spring clothes. West
Thirteenth has loads of trees you'd never suspect in the
winter.... Had dinner with a blind date at a Rumanian restaurant.
It was large, well lit, and noisy as hell. At first, we thought
there was a wedding party going on, but we were wrong—it
was only the usual atmosphere. One man was having a birthday.
They sent drinks over to our table. We've got another date for
Saturday to hit the antique shops on Third. I bought a dress at
Saks to celebrate—lots of ruffles in the front and a straight
skirt—on sale. They come in fits and starts—men, that is! Study
so you can be a God Damned College Gradute!
Love,
Parker

I got up and shut the window. This place needs a poster. I like
faces. It's just a matter of picking the right one. A photograph.

I keep Parker's letters in the dressing room. My chest of drawers is built-in, and I don't have much underwear. The first drawer, in the corner, loose. I just toss them in.

◢ 4

Here I am at the drugstore waiting for some Tedrol. My respiratory system fades just as the weather improves. The doctor said pneumonia three times for emphasis and actually came to my apartment. "I thought house calls were passé!" I tried to sound grateful. "I'm in the Maccabees Building," he said. "Do you have a friend who could stay with you?" I looked away. You don't get hospital insurance with a part-time job.

The landlady brought up my mail. It was long and meaty:

April 15, 1956

Dear Katie,
Thanks so much for sending the pearls, and so quickly, too. I left something everywhere I went that weekend; my mother has been mailing me packages steadily as they've been rounded up.

I was impressed with the Art Museum Founder's Society envelope. I trust your job is as interesting as ever. I would have sold my mother for a part-time job like yours. (How much did you get?)

Love,
Parker

I put the letter down and when I woke up, I had to hurry here before the place closed. Anyway, I'm tempted to call Francis. The nurse always answers the phone. Maybe I could get away with it once more. "You've got a bedridden ex-girlfriend to add to your bedridden wife. Do you think I could have some of her hot lemonade?" What if he makes some excuse? What if? If?

So that's how we got back together. He poured me full of whiskey and shut all the windows and plugged in the vaporizer. He put the sack of lemons in the sink and cut one in half with his pocket knife. The room filled with steam and we ate the lemon, rind and all. I lay there in my underwear and sunk into it. It felt like peace. "I've got to call my boss," I whispered.

"I'll take care of your boss," he said. He put on his coat and went out the door. When he came back, he had a hardcover copy of e. e. cummings, a bottle of Carstairs, and enough Kleenex to go into business. He also had a jar of Vicks salve and some cheesecloth. "Now, let's take care of that lovely chest of yours," he said.

▲ 5

Some Spring!

Dear Parker,

I'm sick in bed, and Francis has found time to deal with that fool I work for and play with me. Everything is better than you might think; but there's no happy ending here, and I don't expect one. I don't want an ending. I want my room and him and pretending, if that's all there is. I know all about what can't be changed.

Francis has given up Pall Malls. "People die of pneumonia," he said. He's had an oxygen tank at home for months, and that never stopped him. So I am consoled.

I know this isn't a real letter.

Love,
Kate

April 27, 1956

Dear Katie,

I hope you're getting a good rest now from that hectic pace of classes, work and keeping up an apartment. Sad as it is to realize, despite our soaring spirits, we do have physical limitations, and to transgress them only brings down the furies.
I trust you're taking advantage of this opportunity to charge your battery (these damned Detroit metaphors!).

I got a new hairstyle—bouffant page boy, which is the devil to keep up, but the change is welcome.

We have several first novels this spring which are very impressive and I'll send you some. I'm writing jacket copy now for all the mysteries and westerns (ugh), but they're easy to do. My most interesting job was to write a jacket for a novel about the love affair between a sculptor and a prostitute. Boy, did I let loose on that one. It's about the Vice Rackets and White Slave Trade in New York, which still goes merrily on even though it's not in the headlines now.

The Editorial Department here is all girls. They float on the latest wind of whatever's current and have no values of their own. I suppose it's the same at other publishers, but right now I like the glamour of being in on everything in the house that you get in Publicity. I should have more definite plans, but I'm satisfied to drift along.

What are your plans for the future? Were you put off by my little speech about New York? Are you still planning to come? How does Francis feel about all this? Getting him to really talk is a feat; I was surprised when you told me about reading to you in bed. Touching. Let's not get too dear! Sentiment cripples the brain, don't you agree? I sound like a quizmaster, but let me know. You are, after all, languishing in a sick bed with time unlimited.

Am sending you a little white number from Barbizon that I

picked up at a discount house. Hope it drives Francis crazy and lifts your spirits. Man does not live by books alone.

Keep your powder dry, m'dear, as they said in the Civil War. I had to move to New York to find the meaning of that quote . . . thought it was face powder, you know, like staying in out of the rain. Well, it's gunpowder! Now figure that out. And just remember this: FRANCIS WILL NEVER GET A DIVORCE. There are other men who read books and who have a few bucks left over to spend on dinner out and Christmas presents.

I figure I've overstepped the boundaries of our friendship; and I'll never do it again—just had three quick beers alone, and I feel old and adrift and terribly lonely. Something, maybe, you can avoid.

Goodnight,
Parker

I may have pneumonia, but I've never been happier: Parker's letter, in spite of its cheap advice, spring outside the window, and Francis's hands. He's in and out all the time, bringing books and flowers. A nap is not just a nap anymore. Since he quit smoking, he talks even more. He's reading *Portrait of a Lady* out loud, a few chapters at a time; and he typed a little poem by Hopkins and put it on my bathroom mirror.

I hate the taste of whiskey, but with lemon and honey, it's not so bad. I haven't felt this relaxed in years. The idea of my boss carrying paintings for those suburban women makes me laugh.

◢7

May 6, 1956

Dear Katie,
I fancy you are on the mend by now—floating around your place
in that batiste nightgown thinking lurid thoughts that don't
match up with it. Seriously, I too have some romantic news.
Have seen a lot of Jack Sloane lately. He's the guy who does a
column in the *Times.* He's submitted a manuscript and has
been bugging me for some word on it. They're Chinese legends,
and he did the translating. He said he learned Chinese
"here and there." Anyway, I'm on good terms with the editor he
submitted them to, and he said I could give a reader's report
on them after the manuscript comes back from the first reader.
Not that it would influence their decision, but I am curious
to see his work. His columns are brilliant in a savage way.
    Have to run for dinner now but will write more later. It's
cold and raining here today, and I hate going out.
                            Love,
                            Parker

    I decided the other day that I like sex too much. It was in the
middle of the night, actually. The vaporizer was on, and the
lemon smell gets a little cloying. I woke Francis up. He had
planned to leave at 2:00 A.M. He slid down the bed and did a
few things that had me gasping for breath. What do I do when
he goes? Living for the moment is okay for morons and drunks,
but the facts are always in the back of my mind; and I want to
crawl up in his lap and say things you won't find in any book. Is
something wrong with me, or do other women feel this too? I
sure won't ask him. And Parker is hopeless. In the meantime, I
hug my pillow, and my hands bring me some relief. I have defi-
nitely got my energy back. On the mend, as Parker says.

◢8

June 3, 1956

Dear Katie,
Went to Coney Island last weekend and what a shining
experience! Acres of human flesh in all sizes and forms jammed
together. You can't help but think of Walt Whitman. He'd
be in his glory here. It stinks humanity, but it's pretty wonderful,
too. No impressions put in words—it's much more than that,
the very stuff of life.

More soon,
Parker

I took a bus to the bookshop and sat in the back and brought
Parker up to date on this miserable manual typewriter. Business
was slow, and Francis read a book. The fans were on.

June 11, 1956

Dear Parker,
I'm back with Francis and out of work. Aced my classes and
enrolled in summer school. Have Shakespeare at 8:30 and
hate it. The teacher's old, has a monotone, and a stiff back.
I'm the only one who's awake, I'm sorry to say. Most of the
plays are recorded at the City Library. Maybe the records will
help. I'm on my way over there now to kill two birds with
one stone. They don't pay much, but they don't fire you either.
Civil Service.

My other class, after supper, is Interpretive Reading.
I took it for the instructor. She reads like someone from
Actor's Studio. She's beautiful, divorced, with sad eyes. She
offered me a research job for a dollar an hour and I had to
refuse.

Francis is not what he seems to be, and I don't know whether
that's good or bad.

Read *The Waves* last week. Tuesday follows Monday, and

19

it all rolls on. How does it feel to be thirty?

We are going on a picnic for my birthday. Have you any advice for me? What comes after Shakespeare? Still job hunting; do you think I could survive in a fork lift office? The pay is good, but it's full-time and the boss weighs three hundred pounds.

Francis has cured my insomnia and complexion. Since I don't have a job yet, I don't need new clothes. White shorts and a few blouses. I gave up haircuts and pin it up now. We're having a heat wave and living on ice tea. My neighbor on the left grows mint in her window box. She sleeps with the barkeep at Lou Walker's, and they make a lot of noise toward morning.

Love,
Kate

I took a bus to the library downtown and filled out another application. The woman there is dried up and hollowed out, but she's not the boss, thank goodness. Shakespeare is not much better recorded. Maybe if Richard Burton tried, he could bring it all to life, but I doubt it. I'm in over my head when I pass the eighteenth century going backwards. I'll never make it as a scholar.

Francis's wife is worse, and he's closing up the shop early. Last night I asked him to walk me to the bus stop; and I got up and waited for him. He affected a steadiness he didn't have, and we left. The radio had just played a piece by Sinatra and he was crying. What do old men see in younger women? Don't tell me their brains, their craziness; and don't add their bodies. I have my own ideas. We're all dying, and men can pretend better with all that fierceness in their arms. Rosy nipples and unblemished skin are beside the point.

◢ 9

July 4, 1956

Dear Katie,

Have not had a chance to write earlier. Been working nights
or seeing people off or going out. Florence and Saul were in,
as you know, with Dante. We went to the Copa and saw Pearl
Bailey. Saw them off on the *United States* (what a boat!).
I wanted to stowaway and go with them.

That next week a couple I know came in on their way to
Europe (for two years—he's a doctor in the Air Force) and
again bon voyage parties. This is between dating the editor and
working two nights a week. I'm just sobering up now and got
a call from Robert tonight. I'm really looking forward to that,
of course, and plan a slam-bang weekend.

Parker

I read Parker's letter and stuffed it in my bag.

August 21, 1956

Dear Parker,

Francis and I walked down to the river, but all that was there was
one freighter. The wrecking ball is never far away, and his
shop goes next. He doesn't talk about it.

Sitting on a bench with Francis bothers me. It's public,
and I'm on fire a lot of the time . . . we act very formal, and sweat
drips off my face. Ninety-eight degrees, and the humidity
is hell. I change clothes twice a day. Still looking for a job
that pays.

Decided to switch my major to Comparative Literature.
Took your advice and sampled a few folks on the continent:
Camus, Sartre and now the Germans. Thomas Mann is the best
of the lot. Can't wait for fall.

Yours,
Kate

◢ 10

Sept. 29, 1956

Dear Parker,

Found a job, and then a second one. Don't faint. It all falls
in place. Here's how: first job is downtown—noon to 5:00.
Receptionist for a hearing-aid salesman. What it amounts to is
answering the phone and stalling off old people who come
in to complain about their expensive "appliances." They are
deaf, and sometimes I have to write them messages on paper.
There's no billing or filing, and that seems odd. Each salesman
takes care of his own, and there are three of them. Long
stretches when the phone doesn't ring and the waiting room
is empty, so I can read. I also run errands, pick up tickets,
go for lunch, etc. The pay is great, and the air-conditioning
works. My boss is polite and preoccupied.

My second job is at a community center playground, four
nights a week. It amounts to babysitting six preschoolers while
they crawl around the cement yard and push baby buggies
full of dolls to the fence. The hours are six to nine. Supper is
free, and the basketball coach gives me a lift home. The kids are
dirty and cute, and their noses run.

My classes are packed in the mornings: Modern Continental
Drama, Art History, French Literature in Translation, Film
History and German. Not a trace of math, science, or P.E.
Francis is helping me with the German, and the professor has
old world charm. The film course amounts to a free movie
twice a week with one text and a critique due every session.
No tests. No long papers. Art History is another pleasure. I
spend Sunday mornings at the City Library on that big leather
couch looking at art books and going over my notes on the
slides. My professor's name is Scheyer and he's famous. The
reading for the lit courses is voluminous. Not a bore in the
bunch, and the buildings are all near Woodward, so I fly downtown on the bus and I'm never late for anything! It's enough

to make you believe in God, but I don't.

I read all weekend at the library or in bed. Francis is nobody to depend on . . . he calls and writes . . . but he's all voice and words. . . . First the Bookseller's in Boston, then his son to Dartmouth, then a crazy trip for books to Maine, an estate sale . . . he looks older every time I see him. His wife is the same, but he can't afford the nurse in the evenings, now. So he stays home. I'm lucky if I see him once a week, and then it's at the shop. I type my papers there. He actually made love to me (between customers) standing up. It was exciting, but humiliating when my brains came back to Earth. I drew the line at that point.

He hasn't seen my apartment since I painted it glossy pink and put up two posters: one is Marlene Dietrich in a top hat and black tie. It's huge, and I love it. The paint was free. The new landlady is a reasonable person, and I bought the posters with my first paycheck! I am an independent woman.

Still have this lousy cough. Hope you are out and about. I decided to have a Christmas party. I believe in advance planning. Do you like eggnog?

Forward,
Kate

◢11

October 10, 1956

Dear Parker,

You asked for my favorite cummings poem, but it's on the wall,
and you'll see it at my party. Francis will meet you at the
airport. Wait for him. He's late to everything these days.
The poem is haunting; at least it haunts me. I never take
psychology courses and make no bones about tripping up
people who get lost in that jargon at parties. "My analyst," my
foot! Usually they are seeing somebody's sister with a Master's
degree and enough pomposity to fill a room with cathedral
ceilings. Nobody I know can afford a psychiatrist, let alone
an analyst. That's another thing insurance doesn't cover.
I'm beginning to sound like a union man. It's this city. "You can
run, but you can't hide"; Joe Louis said that. He wasn't
talking about automobiles, but he might as well have been.
He is a Detroiter. Our own! And he learned everything the
hard way.

My paperboy drinks gin. Eleven years old. He runs errands
for me when I'm sick. More on the charms of YOUR city.
MY city is not charming. You see the plays, and I'll read the
books . . . until I get out of here and get a real job.

The hearing-aid rep is cheating the old people. He's slick,
and rich, and without a scruple. But he's quiet when I'm around,
and he gave me a big raise Friday. He also buys my lunch.
"Get one for yourself," he yells. So I'm living on salami and
rye and ice water. I make the same with these two jobs as I did at
the museum, but this time around, I get meals and no glamour.

It doesn't take a genius to see I'm selling my soul for this
degree, and Francis seems to own my body—though all he ever
bought for me were a few lemons and a vaporizer. Tell me
this: Can my mind be free when, in the middle of a lecture
on German verbs, I dream of writhing in his arms and my panties
are wet?

We flew a kite at Rouge Park Sunday afternoon and almost made love in the bushes. Francis is less and less formal.
I bought a long khaki shirt—thick cotton, and I've stopped wearing underpants. "Terribly convenient, m'dear." We live a decadent life in this frontier town . . . once a week. Even writing about it excites me.

Love,
Kate

October 28, 1956

Parker,
Have been reading more of the hardcover copy of e. e. cummings Francis gave me. The poems are numbered and cummings has kissed punctuation good-bye. Go to the library and read #197.

Now, doesn't that poem make psychology look like the ugly nest of worms that it is? What can those graybeards tell you about suicide that even gets close to what cummings has to SHOW? The chairman of the English Department shot himself this morning. Nobody knows why, and everybody loved him.

Love and faith,
Kate

December 26, 1956

Dear Parker,
Here I am at the typewriter with a stack of paper. It's snowing
hard. Francis is mailing out a box of books to his son. You'd
think they didn't have bookstores in New Hampshire! His
catalog is back from the printer, and he's in the middle of
that mailing too. He's off to the post office before it closes,
so I have time for a few words. I have no idea where we're going
for supper, or if we're even going to eat together.

Yesterday was tough. I slept late and had breakfast at the
S & C Diner. I've lost interest in waffles and mankind, as well as
the morning edition, even a free one. In twenty minutes,
I was back in my bathrobe. Of course, Francis didn't call.
The libraries were closed. The museum, too. I listened to the
radio all afternoon with the window wide open and the pipes
knocking. I don't pay the heat, so it was fun to be reckless.

The Israeli student and his girlfriend knocked on my door
at 3:00 and invited me down for a drink. I dug out a clean
pair of black wool pants and put on a red sweater, a little tribute
to the season, and walked on in.

We finished off a jug of wine and a plate of hamburgers.
They have a record player and a stack of Edith Piaf. At first
I kept my mouth shut and listened. When the conversation
turned to Paris, I asked questions and settled back and listened
some more. So now I have a real neighbor. When I went back to
my apartment, I wrote an effusive thank you and closed the
window.

Now it can be told. Francis and I are having cold stuffing
for supper and washing it down with Crown Royal, a gift from
the Canadian publisher's rep. I am ravenous. Too bad you're
not here to appreciate the whiskey. It all tastes the same to me,
but I like the burning feeling in my throat and the effects.

My mother sent me a pair of sturdy nylons and a hot pad.

I threw them in the trash. I told Francis not to bother with a present, and we got into a fight. That was a week ago. He told me I needed to eat two meals in a row so maybe he'd wrap a sirloin steak in a red ribbon. Am I becoming part of the real and everyday?

Merry Christmas,
Kate

▲13

Jan. 7, 1957

Dear Parker,

On New Year's Eve, we had a rare bit of luxury. Edith Piaf and some champagne. Francis put the record in brown wrap and taped it with a pink Dickensian Christmas card with a punch bowl and a banner draped across the groaning board. The champagne came from Shields' downstairs. He and Francis have a lot in common; their rooms are literally being ripped from under them.

A lot of worn-out boxers hang out there, and the lights are too bright, but you can't beat it for convenience and the drinks were free. We'd still be there, if Shields had had his way; Francis had to take the bus home. He was d-r-a-i-n-e-d. I was a bit unrestrained in my reaction to the gift. I think I surprised him. His clothes were a mess, and we knocked over a lamp.

By the way, what do you think of Edith Piaf?

Happy New Year,
Kate

P.S. Are you interested in my courses for the new semester? Or has life there taken you beyond such things? The engineering student from Israel broke up with his girlfriend. He was a messenger boy during the Holocaust. I didn't ask him what that entailed. He was nine years old at the time. We talk in the hall, and he needs a new coat.

◢14

Jan. 23, 1957

Dear Katie,

How silly of you to apologize for saying how you feel. I've been in the same gloomy state of mind myself since I returned home from Christmas, so if we complain to one another, perhaps it will act as a purge.

Your weekend sounded pretty good, what with the snowball fight and all. I still can't believe Francis gave up smoking; what a moral influence you are—in spite of your torrid sex life! It will take me months before I get rid of the image of him emerging from a cloud of smoke in his stinking three-piece suits.

Just found out my grandmother has lung cancer, and she's still working in the school cafeteria at Sacred Heart trying to get her full pension. You can't tell me there's not a connection. Until I was seven years old, I thought she was born with a Camel stuck in her mouth. Filthy habit.

We have been living the most disgustingly wholesome life for the past few weeks. "We" are those without dates. I'm so tired of the company of the same sex, at work and after. I've been working overtime quite a bit to get money for my brother's wedding, so things have been grim.

I have new duties on the job now—no more letters and will handle advance galleys and review copies and pictures and bios, and perhaps some more book jacket covers.

Robert Penn Warren was in last week, and so was Ayn Rand, who struck me as rather odd. Had a ticklish phone call from William Carlos Williams this week; he's getting forgetful and sent this confused card. I had to find out what he meant, and turned out to be too late to do what he wanted—send some books where he was giving a lecture. It's pathetic to see a mind like his gradually fade from age, and worse, he's aware of it. Enough of name dropping.

I can't wait to see you. How clever to check the bulletin board for a ride, and to actually find one. All you need pay for is drink. Let's live on hors d'oeuvres the whole time! My present misanthropic state is directed primarily toward my landlady. She's tried to take me under her ratty wing and has been a regular pest lately. Have a lot to say, but it will be better talking in person.

Ta-Ta,
Parker

◢15

Feb. 10, 1957

Dear Parker,
The trip is off. Had another spell of coughing and hacking
and ran a high fever. Took my trip money to pay Dr. Mossman
and he told me to stay in bed and cut class, if I can't miss
work. So I sleep late and don't go anywhere on the weekends.
Francis is preoccupied. My fever is down, and so am I.

Yours,
Kate

◢ 16

March 29, 1957

Dear Katie,

Sorry I couldn't come over, but it was a fast two days. My flight back from the funeral started off with a bang. I sat on the plane next to a handsome young man, and we talked all the way in. He's from Worcester, Mass. and, as he had a two-hour layover at La Guardia, he suggested we have some refreshments; and we did. We exchanged addresses and he said he'd be coming to New York. He's nice, but get this—he works for an undertaker. I just don't know!

Took a trip on the Staten Island Ferry and froze my ass—determined to see it all.

Called a friend who works for *Time*, and we had dinner and went to see *The Misanthrope* by Moliere in a circle-in-the-round theater (translation by Richard Wilbur, who was at Wayne last spring). The play was one of the most delightful things I've ever seen. This was its second night, and if it's still playing when you come, we must go see it. Don't give up.

That's been my big social life so far. Haven't been to a single bar. New York has been heady enough—a cheap drunk, you must admit.

Let me know what's going on, by all means, and I mean soon, sooner.

Say hello to Francis for me. Whatever else you two are, you seem to have a corner on devotion. Two fanatics.

This is your old, lonesome, respectable, sober buddy.

Parker

I met the minister at the community center today; he wears built-up shoes and races on the dead run from room to room with his fat secretary at his side, thinking she has found God! And, he is trying to convert me. I asked him point-blank if he was going to fire me for not believing. He looked a little put off and said no. I continued eating my supper, which was 90 percent grease but filling. Why is Detroit so full of the South? I know the answer to that one. Why did I ask the question? I wish people would just leave me alone. Anyway, he's not going to fire me, and that's all I care about.

The two hearing-aid salesmen/junior partners (as they are called) asked me out. Separate but equal—both fools. I'm getting sick of salami on rye.

▲17

Still Spring

Dear Katie,
Been reading Dostoyevsky and Flaubert for relief from
Random's dim-witted recent books. They both have great things
ahead of them if they keep up this good writing.
I'd say more, but it's late. Answer this immediately and let
me know the latest. If you see Francis, tell him there were
no galleys on *The Town*—books were ready so early. Say hello to
everyone, and nothing in excess and some things not at all.
Parker

    I got Parker's note this morning. Saturday is my favorite day,
and I read it with coffee at the Student Center. I guess it's time
to read a little Faulkner. I tried once before—the one about the
bear—and it was boring. Hunting has always seemed like a
waste of time and money. Sitting, waiting, looking at a tree,
knowing you will kill and brag about it. The novels are really
hard. So I took out *Light in August* on the librarian's whim. I
think I'll surprise Francis with my direction. Sometimes I feel so
green; he has done so much and been so many places. Without
much money, too, but before his life caved in. Before the accident. Living in New York makes so much possible. Sometimes I
get jealous of him and Parker and disgusted with myself for
surrendering to such ugly feelings.

May 24, 1957

Dear Parker,
There isn't much latest to let you know. It's Saturday, and I make
my way from library to library, one with those wonderful
cubicles; and the white marble city library with its upholstered
furniture and nooks and crannies. I'm sitting in a wing chair

right now looking over the balcony wishing I had the whole evening with Francis. As it is, he's coming by at ten when he gets off the train. He's been up your way.

I'm trying to read *Light in August* this weekend, so I can be ready for the newest Faulkner. Isn't *The Town* part of a trilogy? Think there will be galleys on the others? It is so exciting to be in on these perks. I'll give Francis the message.

I thought your advice was stupid. Everything good must be done in excess. How about a longer letter?

Kate

June 30, 1957

Dear Katie,

Got your list of classes and complaints. After that piece of
heaven you had last semester, what with even a job sans boss
around, to read novels undisturbed—you can expect a few
disappointments.

It's really too bad about DeLaney. He is likeable, but he
always plays to the galleries. Don't let Tennyson's asinine
performance as Man Thinking make you underestimate him
as a poet. He was one, regardless; at least I enjoyed some of his
things just for that. I've always regretted how they didn't
have any Comparative Lit courses; and now you're getting in
on the ground floor. Three out of five ain't bad. German is
hard for EVERYONE. Just a question: How come you are in
Victorian Lit, anyway? You have more than enough English
credits. Did you take it just because it's in the morning?

Finally have my phonograph, but when I plugged it in for the
first time, it started smoking. I thought it was going to burst
into flames. It's this damned D/C current, I suppose, one of
the lesser joys of living in quaint, old buildings.

Work has been at such a frantic pace lately, I walk around
in a daze. I can't describe it, but I'm beginning to yearn for
quieter pastures than Publicity. The bug has been put in my
ear by several people at Random lately. First (brag coming),
Saxe Commins, Faulkner's editor, told me last week he wished I
was his secretary, but that it would be awkward switching.
I'd really love that, and I'd be in pure editorial work, but nothing
can be done, now. Then, one of the lesser women editors
and I had some confidential talks, and she urged me to apply for
a job outside Random. She outlined things pretty thoroughly
and knew what she was talking about. Hope you don't mind my
rambling on so about something that must be so uninteresting
to you, but it's been on my mind so lately, and I don't know

what to do.

This girl is very interesting; and my God, is she "learned"! She gave me the lowdown on Columbia's Lit Department, Trilling, et al. (doesn't like them) and knows all these fabulous intellectuals around town like Barzun and Riesman. She's just been offered a job at *Mademoiselle* as their Associate Fiction Editor. But turned it down because of all the Smith-Wellesley chi-chi crap you have to turn out, so I'm impressed.

No dates lately, alas, Robert hasn't called since I got back; so that's it. Commins's secretary and I, however, did stop for "one" after work Friday, wound up at her apartment for "more" (she lives with her father, so it's quite an establishment), then flew down to Julius's, which was packed in honor of St. Patrick and had a ball. Met one boy who was fairly decent, but his face lit up too much when he found out I lived alone, so I stayed with the gang. That sounds rather prim, doesn't it? But it's always a factor, it seems, here. It even ceases to be amusing, after a while.

Your party was really great, and I only wish again, that I had been in a better condition to appreciate it. Could certainly use one now.

I loved your apartment. You've made pink into something beyond girlish. Maybe it's the gloss; maybe it's what isn't in it. Not much, you must admit! For Christ's sake, buy a chair. Hope you liked all those pillows. My mother covered them. NOBODY SHOULD HAVE TO SIT ON A BOARD! Seriously, what I like most is that photo of Marlene D. It's so big, and so much is in it. Get rid of those cummings poems—don't you think you've outgrown them? As Man Feeling, he goes a long way; but as Man Thinking he loses out. We all have our preferences—and, anyway, the paper looks ratty. Everything else looks so clean and spare; and I love your desk. Doesn't anyone notice it's missing from the bookshop? That family is tight as ticks; don't be fooled; and Francis's son isn't on a full scholarship because he's stupid!

I only talk like this when I've had a few, and I have had a few. Oh, Katie, think of yourself a little. How long can this go on? Francis is coming to the Bookseller's next month and wants me to get tickets to something funny. How unlike him not to have a play picked out, a real play. I think the whole LIE is beginning to get to him. There is nothing funny in town.

I thought about the circus, but we all know what clowns really are. I talk big, but when I sober up, it slips away.

I just would like to spare you some pain. Isn't there enough for you—without Francis?

This is your garrulous, pushy, well-meaning buddy thanking you for everything. Without your letters, my evenings would be flatter and blacker.

Forever,
Parker

P.S. Thanks for the soma. I have the curse and this is the worst of all worlds. I hate apple pie and dogs, and everyone—regardless of race or creed, right now; and those pills may prevent an antisocial crime. Let me know any late news from the provinces.

P.P.S. I also hate Shakespeare, Adlai Stevenson, beer parties, and rich women.

Parker

◢19

July 14, 1957

Dear Katie,

Well, how the hell are you? It was so good talking to you the other night, especially since I've been planning to call you but the money part deterred my fine intentions. Am home from work today due to a king-sized hangover, my first in a month, so don't feel too guilty about it—in fact, it's fun now as I'm still high as a kite at three in the afternoon. OUR FRIEND, FRANCIS, rang my doorbell at 11:30 last night, and we buzzed out for a few. Don't remember what time I came in, don't remember getting in, as far as that goes. What a day! The plumber has been in twice, my landlady once, so I find, but I don't remember letting them in!

We (Francis, not the plumber) went to this bar next door to my place and talked for hours with the bartender (former model, actor, and painter) and another guy who's a poet and student of Far Eastern philosophy. After we got the bartender to close up, as he was spilling the drinks, we went over to the other guy's apartment and guzzled some more in front of the fireplace. Now, I'm just fine up to there, but things are a blank after that. But, here I am, virginally intact, so I guess everything's okay.

Didn't get a chance to talk with Francis, but he looked pretty good. Good grief! The plumber's in again, and I'm dying to conk out and can't. I feel pretty lousy right now, as you can see. This is a very impressionistic letter.

Six P.M. Went to the doctor with an eye infection, after sleeping all day. Let me hear from you. And soon. And love. And tell Francis I appreciate the books. They are indeed rare and so is he!

Parker

"Francis, here I am going on twenty-three years old, and the same old stuff is floating around in my head."

"What are you talking about?" Francis is lying on the studio couch in the back room of his new shop reading the *Times*. It's Sunday afternoon, and he'll be opening up in an hour.

"Come here, Katherine."

Before you know it, his hands are around my waist, and he is kneeling on the floor. "I don't like this, Francis. I want you to hold me." It's hard not to fall off the couch. His fingers are inside me, and his words are loud.

"Don't open the shop," I whisper.

"Do you want more, more, Katie, a little more? How about a little slower, Katie, wait a little, Katie." His hands are on my hips, and he's breathing so hard I have trouble hearing his words. He's not loud now.

"I want it, Francis, I want enough of it, don't leave me all hot and dying while you show somebody a book! Make it last, make me crazy." And he is a little too fierce. I bite his shoulder to keep from screaming. The walls are thin, and his landlady lives next door in the back of a tailor shop. What miserable luck.

But I am wrong. He puts on his pants and goes out front and pulls the shades. He pulls the phone cord and takes what's left of the Crown Royal out of his closet. "All right, Katherine." I still have my blouse and bra on, and my nylons are around my ankles. "Sit on my lap, love," he says.

Who could refuse him? He mashes his face in my breasts and I think of all the hours left; and, do you know, he keeps right on going farther down; and I'm not saying it was the first time; he wasn't hard right away, and he said, "I'm going to rub you till you don't want it anymore; and maybe you'll walk around the room and let an old man see that lovely chest of yours. Don't you think I want to forget the rest of my life, Katherine? Don't you think I want more than one afternoon?"

His hands are on my lips, and my legs are wide. I really don't care about the lady next door. I don't care.

◢21

August 6, 1957

Dear Parker,

Francis is telling me what I can't quite hack. The Master's goes nowhere. What does go? He's told me I don't have a prayer with a college teaching job because I'm a woman—even with a Ph.D. He can rattle off all the deadends and the hellavit is he's right. The department chairman said the same thing— they feel obliged to point out reality, liberal arts is not for the liberal, it's for the rich! Francis agrees. I was so flattered to get the fellowship that I stopped thinking for awhile, and that is fatal.

Anyway, I'm not leaving Francis for New York, and where else does publishing pay a living wage? San Francisco with the pseudo everything, avant-garde barbarians? I had enough of the real thing, growing up. No thanks. That leaves me with easy choices. In town. On the busline. I don't even want a transfer. There are no wonderful jobs in Detroit. So I've settled on a library. Secure. Automobiles are outside the doors. I DON'T CARE WHAT ELSE IS INSIDE. My fellowship is all freshman composition. I hate teaching grammar, correcting illiterate papers, and seeing all the poor kids who aren't going to make it.

So, I'm finishing out the semester, collecting my check, and beginning a Master's in library science, come fall. I deserve a little security, so I can live and read. Francis wanted me to finish up the first degree before starting the second, but I can't see it. "Katherine, you have time; and they are paying you," he gets a little angry. I'd never tell him, but I keep thinking he might die in the middle of it all. I've got to have something solid in my life, a real job with insurance and vacations. And silence. Nobody is taking my life—what's left of it—anyway!

I have other news. The nurse is back in the evenings, and his son got a job in the Chem Lab at Dartmouth. We have supper out once in a while. You know, corner tables and waiters at the ready. And, Francis has upgraded his brand of whiskey! I thought that was all until he brought me a box wrapped in his ever-ready brown paper. I pulled out a pink flannel nightgown and some pink satin slippers—the kind with high heels and pompoms—the kind nobody wears—except in fantasy land! That's not all. A brass candle holder and a fat pink candle. The note read: "Time for a little nightlife, Katherine!"

"Don't die, Francis." I threw myself in his arms.

"Well, I'll be damned. Is that how you react to a windfall?" And he carried me to the shower and turned on the warm water. My dress was plastered to my body and I was laughing so hard, I nearly choked. He peeled off my clothes, piece by piece, and said: "I see you need some instruction in having fun."

He was right.

Love,
Kate

P.S. Now Francis stays over at least twice a week—all night—and we eat oranges for breakfast and go out for coffee. I wouldn't call it ordinary and I wouldn't call it wild, but there's not a name for everything. I love him so much I told him so. He didn't say anything at first. And then he said I'd better start reading to him because he was getting older, and his eyes were going. The next day a copy of *Women in Love* was in my mail box. Are we back to D. H. Lawrence, Parker? Francis has new glasses now, and he looks very literary!

If all happy families are alike, does that hold true for lovers? I think I will use the word again.

Write soon, sooner, soonest.
Kate

◢22

August 18, 1957

Dear Kate,

Francis doesn't look literary. He tries. Three-piece suits. That old briefcase. Come on!

I'm glad you're happy. I can't imagine you a librarian. Can you spend your whole life posing? But you're right, short of revolution, it's a steady job—ANYWHERE. Another advantage, the hours can be switched; and women move around and can bide their time. A job like that frees you up. Play your cards right, and you can walk to work.

Is that Israeli engineer still in your building? How old is he? Nothing sounds more boring than engineering, but his history... I dream about it.

Am watching a James Mason movie, *A Star Is Born.* His voice paralyzes me and he makes a marvelous drunk. Very angry. "I'm as sober as a judge, and I know exactly what I'm saying." He wears tailored pajamas as if they were de rigeur. Judy Garland sings and breathes, but she can't act.

So far, tonight, I have washed my hair, done my nails, ironed a blouse, blown a fuse (a real one), and baked a cake.

Tell me about Henry James . . . you left him in midair a few months back (I have also reread your letters); I like his lines and pace, but his sentences are too complicated. The plots are tough, too.

I'm forging on, penniless and alone, through his novels, in spite of everything. *Daisy Miller* is first—short enough, too.

The movie is over—Judy Garland is a twit.

Love,
Parker

◢ 23

Dear Parker,
I am sitting in the sun on the new bench outside the new bookshop. There's a lot of construction on campus these days. Ugly. Uniform. No pattern to it. The classrooms have no windows, but the halls do. Figure that one out. I'm sure the architect has. Something to do with distractions. More like traps.
　I feel rotten, but I don't know why. It's not fall, yet everything feels dead.
　Cheer me up, can you?

Friends to the grave,
Kate

Feb. 29, 1958

Dear Katie,

I feel conscience-bound to level with you. I have three of the
worst problems a woman could have. I'm pregnant, I lost my
job, and the father of the child is married. I might add that
I am a fool, but that is implied, don't you think?

If I stick to the facts, I'll be all right. I'm doing something
about the first problem before I come back, and I'm coming back
in two weeks. My flight is booked, and what little furniture
I had is sold. Nobody knows but you, and if you tell Francis,
you can forget our friendship.

I'm not telling the father because I hate him. It's that simple.
You certainly understand, don't you? Negotiate and compromise
don't seem to be your favorite words either.

I will be staying with my mother until I find a job downtown. I
know you and Francis can help me look for an apartment.
I want something new and beautiful. It won't be hard to find a
secretarial job that pays; after all, it was those skills that
landed me the niche at Random; without them, Francis's
connections would have been pretty little frills. All I'm hoping
for is a decent man to work for; if the job itself is a bore, I
could care less. Thank God, there's no recession.

I see things pretty straight these days; and one thing I know is I
can't live without hope of a marriage. Kids I can forget, but
I don't handle the single life with any grace; and frankly,
I'm drinking so much it's a wonder the baby didn't float out
in a flood of martinis! The only reason I don't drink before noon
on the weekends is I sleep till one o'clock. And that's because
I have a hangover both mornings.

It's all a circle. It's hard to remember birth control when
you're blistered on cheap gin. My new boss drinks too, a fatal
combo at lunch. Overtime, tension, "I have to relax," I said
to myself. I was relaxed all right. I didn't get these sterling

insights out of my own head. A little help, as they say. Fifty
dollars an hour plus a few pills and a referral in Detroit!
  Goodbye to the city. It's going to be hard to shift gears, but
here I am already back in Detroit metaphors!
  Now make up something to tell Francis; he's been a real friend,
but he'll never be an intimate. Get busy and read the ads for
high rises so you can be an expert when I get in. By the way,
when are you moving out of that Murphy bed? Isn't it time?
Six months into a Master's with a fellowship. Dear me, where are
your priorities? This is an age of materialism. It's one thing
to ride the bus, but you go too far.
  Thank you, Katie, for everything.
Love,
Parker

◢ 25

Another Spring

Dear Katie,

Thought you'd want to hear the latest when I had a free
evening to get it down on paper. I can't seem to get you on
the phone. Am working for an Irish politician. Writing some
speeches, doing a little P.R., but mostly it's letters and the
phone. He's a little harsh and he drinks, but he's basically
decent. He never asks me why I order Vernor's, and the bonuses
keep coming.

I'm keeping my social life on hold. I've taken up bowling.
It doesn't take brains, just concentration. Remember what
Francis used to say of his last months in New York, after the
accident, how he felt knocking the pins down. The only time
I ever heard him talk about his anger. Well, he was right.
It helps. It's hard to get an alley, if you're not in a league,
but I manage.

Am having floor to ceiling bookcases put in my apartment.
Met the carpenter who's doing it in a philosophy class.
All those Tuesday nights, and we finally went out for a drink
when the last class was over. He's gay, but he does great work,
and sometimes we have dinner together at his place.

What's up?

Love,
Parker

PART TWO

Death and the Fat Man

◢ 1

It was a streak of good fortune, and for a while everything fit into it—an upward trend, so to speak. We felt freer; I guess money does that if you let it. It bought us time. We took walks up Cass Avenue after Francis closed the shop, and we had drinks in the bar at Lelli's and ordered the antipasto. I love the stucco walls and the wishing well and the waiters in their tuxedos. It's a mix—secretaries and their bosses from the GM Building, Italian families, and a few bachelors who live in the two-story apartments on Grand Boulevard.

The weather had a bite to it that fall; I wore a navy surplus sweater with my wool slacks, and it felt good. Two nights a week, with Francis, turned into three, with the third an alarm-clock setter. We made all kinds of plans for a weekend in New York, but something always came up. The plans themselves seemed enough. It was all so much better than what we had.

We bought things—a wall of battered-up bookcases at a junk shop—and we painted them; baby oil and bubble bath, and we used it up fast and bought more; we sat around the shop during the week reading and talking. The homework in library science is a joke—three hours a day and it's done. I read what I wanted in the evenings. Once we were back in my apartment, Francis asked me to take off my bra, but leave my sweater on. Nowadays, run-of-the-mill behavior, but I felt wanton, then, even behind closed doors. He liked to talk about sex as much as carry it through, and I was mesmerized. In the end, my sweater would be shoved up to my shoulders, and his mouth didn't stop. I wasn't hot and dying anymore! I felt full.

◢ 2

I was in the middle of rereading *The Waves*, trying to focus on the solid parts—hang the words there—when a passage jumped out and clamped me in a sweat. Powerful words.

But if one day you do not come after breakfast, if one day I see you in some looking-glass perhaps looking after another, if the telephone buzzes and buzzes in your empty room, I shall then, after unspeakable anguish, I shall then—for there is no end to the folly of the human heart —seek another, find another, you. Meanwhile, let us abolish the ticking of time's clock with one blow. Come closer.

I'm not like that. I won't find another. Maybe I'll die before Francis does. My age is no insurance, and he's not sick. Why do I think about it so much, dream it? Everything's so private now. I feel breathless—not from the sex—from the anticipation of his stories, his comparisons; yes, sex, too, from the teasing, the words. Soft, like a lullaby: "Katherine," . . . his hands are under my skirt, moving, and his voice follows . . . "come for me, Katherine," his fingers are fluttering; I shut my eyes tight and feel he is watching my face. "My little animal . . . you want it, Katie, Katie; so wet, Katie; come for me. . . ."

"Please don't leave me, Francis." He mashes his mouth on mine, and his tongue and hands seem the same. I don't know why I cry. His concern for me—a wild woman—I love him and it. I love the messiness, the stickiness, and I stretch and try to get my breath back. His arm is propped up: "You know, Katie, kissing can be more intimate than sex, don't you think? No, I guess you don't," and he smiles and holds my hand. By the time my voice comes back and my brain follows, I ask him for a glass of water.

This, I think, is the beginning of old age. If we were arguing in a classroom, I could see his point, but this is a life of pillows and screams: "It's all intimate to me. I guess you think more about yourself in the last part, right before you come, than when you're kissing. Is that what you mean?"

"Close enough," he says. His voice is low.

"Katie, you deserve someone younger, who could go on all night, and there's no end to my selfishness, you know that, don't you?" And he hugs me tight enough to break me in half. He's the one in tears now, the only time I have ever seen him cry. My mouth is dry, but I forget about the water.

"It's like he wasn't here. He saved the best for you. All the words. I knew something was up when he quit smoking. It just didn't make sense. And he didn't lie about it. 'I just quit,' he said. We had been after him to quit for years. It was a family joke. He smoked so much . . . then he was quiet, preoccupied. You sure have brass to come here. My mother was beautiful—you look ordinary. Plain." He kicked the fish tank.

We were in the little waiting room close to the machines and patients—hardly big enough for four chairs—alone. I expected worse, to be ignored, to be called names. So I sat. What could I say? His son is a golden boy; at least he looks like one. Ivy League, all the things I hate. I don't hate him, it's just like everything, so different than you'd been led to believe.

I saw the blinds drawn in his shop that Monday, and I knew something awful had happened. The nurse at home told me the details, Harper's, critical.

I was the first to come. The doctor was in the nursing station charting. "I'm his mistress. I want the truth." The nurses did a double take, and the doctor took my arm. "A day or two," he said. I guess he was the resident; Parker thinks so, but you know how they usually talk around everything and stare at the wall? Well, this one didn't. "I'm not coming back," I said. But I did. And that's how I met his son.

I left my imprint in the doctor's hands, but he didn't flinch. He walked me to the room, all the machines and lights and the nurses and their white crispness, and Francis, pale and sleeping with bars at his side and an IV in his arm. That was my funeral, that was it, the resident didn't say any more.

I walked straight back to my apartment; it's not a safe neighborhood. School was letting out. A few eight-year-olds teased me: "What are you doing, lady?" I took their question to heart. I passed those jazz clubs on John R, and they don't look so good in the daytime. I turned at the side of the art museum and rounded the corner of the Maccabees Building, and, on an impulse, went up the elevator to Dr. Mossman's office. "I've got to see him," I said. Nobody was in the waiting room, but the receptionist said the examining rooms were full. He walked out of one, slamming the door like he does, and looked·up. "Please," I said and threw myself at him. Dr. Mossman pushed me into his office and gave me a glass of water. Then he waited. "Francis might as well be dead, all I want is sleeping pills, I can't stand this, I can't stand it!" He prescribed three and wrote his home phone number on a slip of paper. "Katherine, I won't lecture you." That's all he said.

There was nothing to buy at the drugstore after I got the three pills. Death is not like a bad cold.

When I walked in the door of my apartment and locked it, I picked up the phone and called Parker. "I'll be over as soon as I tell my boss what happened. Take a bath." I can count on her for some stupid advice. Instead, I took a set of dishes and broke it, piece by piece, in the sink. Does that make any sense to you? I never cried again that day, and I wasn't crying then. What else did I do? I left town and stopped writing letters to anybody for a long time. I also missed Parker's wedding, but I have a snapshot of her under the chupa with the Israeli engineer at her side.

◢ 4

On Friday nights, after the clerk walks out of the library door and the janitor shoves his resin can in the back room closet, I feel a rush of anticipation for the twenty minutes before I, too, leave the library. There is little to do. The football games pull away the students and housewives, and most old people have left by then for supper. So the thud of the stamper—we have not been changed by any lighted computer that photographs numbers—and the smell of ink, overpowered by the tea olive blossom on my desk, tell a tale of tradition, not efficiency.

My clerk this year is a tall boy with girlish blond looks. He wears white shirts with buttoned-down collars and what used to be Sears khaki pants. He doesn't say much, but he does exactly what I tell him, after he asks to have it repeated. Nobody has ever tried so hard not to make a mistake.

I thought I had discovered the new clerk's darkest secret when I saw him in Detroit, one weekend at the beginning of the term, dressed in satin heels and gauze pants held together at the ankle by thick rubber bands. His long arms were covered by a cape, and only the pale hair on his wrists gave any indication of his manhood.

I have never known another transvestite, though there is a short story set in Scotland about a married woman who is his literary counterpart. I cried at the end when her husband discovers her in the wide lapel suit she used for years in fantasy games with their three children. Her temporary transformation had been so successful that the neighbors who spied thought she was carrying on with another man. They stayed together after the inevitable confrontation. Small towns don't offer much choice. And that's exactly why I picked Lapeer.

The clerk and I—his name is Lesley—have settled in for the promise of four years of arranging and rearranging. He is a freshman, and the only clerk who did not stay till graduation died in a car wreck after we won the 1961 football championship.

These sharpened pencils on my desk are for show; a felt tipped pen, royal blue, does the real work. The late October sun comes through these high windows, and it changes the mahogany paneling, the dust in the air, and the hardwood floors in that twenty minutes before dusk comes. Next Friday I will again sit at this desk, and bittersweet will have replaced the tea olive in the cracked bowl.

The only friend I allow myself, Parker, lives in Detroit. Parker is still there, downtown, married; let's not go into that. Since I came here, I have been careful to maintain just the right amount of weight. Men don't bother me in that way anymore. I am free to read. When the library's new arrivals have been consumed, when paperback swap shops yield nothing, I spend the evening knitting; and, once a year, spend a long weekend in New York City. I save no money. My clothes are old. My walls bare. I have limited my pleasure to reading; and such a restriction requires vigilance, just as it is a thin line not to balloon up to the kind of obesity doctors warn against or stop eating altogether.

The truth revealed itself gradually and I held each new part of it in my head, waiting for the sum as if it could decide for me what to do. Yet, all along, I knew I would "do" nothing. I watched Lesley work and heard him laugh. He waited before he responded to a joke, and he laughed longer than the others. He watched me. At first I thought it was his secret life in those flimsy clothes that made him cautious. But gradually, after noticing his slow, careful lettering, his absorption in stamping and gluing, the unfocused look in his eyes, the truth entered my thoughts and remained in my dreams.

He stacked the magazines, first on a chair, then in the rack, checking slowly what another would have hurried through. He absently touched the leather bindings in the rare book section. He watched the shavings from an eraser drift in the air. The whir of the typewriter was enough to absorb him while he waited, on a slow Saturday, at the checkout desk. I had thought him shy, a good listener; now I wondered how much he understood of the questions the patrons asked, of the conversations he overheard.

In December, he began wearing turtleneck sweaters. He had two: chocolate brown and navy. A more solid look. He ate his lunch in the same chair every day. He listened to records after work on Saturdays. Soon what worried me was the thought he might leave. I had grown used to his softness and his poignant, almost deceptive attempt to ape others.

When I checked around town, I discovered Lesley lived with his brother, Charley, who works nights at a factory. The two of them moved here in August and rented a flat not far from the library.

Quiet, careful not to intrude, Lesley did his job. I had, always before, been repelled by dumb people, but now I longed to throw my head in his lap, to touch his soft cheeks. I, too, cannot learn the signs, the jokes, though I laugh on cue and understand all the punch lines.

I fell in love with Lesley's softness and beauty. Seduced by the emptiness and innocence in his eyes. Preoccupied by the nature of dumbness itself, I watched him, without seeming to. He kept a cut-out strip of the alphabet folded in his pocket; the upper and lower case letters were colored in alternating shades of purple and pale blue. I watched him looking at the calendar when the checkouts let up. He has tried to memorize the library!

Little by little, alphabetical order slipped by us both. I corrected his mistakes. Gradually my concern for him seeped into the safety I had made here. I could see in his eyes the hope that he was guessing right when he was forced to hurry. I let him stay late to finish what another clerk would have sandwiched between the phone calls and the stamp-ins.

Today Lesley told me my hair looked like Rapunzel's straw. He surprises me with phrases like that, and I wonder about his childhood. I imagine him wrapped in a quilt or comforter, as we call them here in the Midwest. In my fantasy, his mother reads his fairy tales, one by one, over and over, until the words, the images are captured, at last, by his slow mind.

◢ 5

Oct. 18, 1962

Dear Kate,

Every time I think of you stuck in that apartment in that
God-forsaken town with second-rate Victorian porches
distracting people from the real horrors, every time I think
of any of it, I feel my blood pressure rise; and if I still drank,
I'd be on my second one. How anyone, let alone you, could
choose to go there is beyond me. Lapeer, please!

Don't send me any more pictures. You look awful, and it's no
wonder. What is there to do besides eat and read? We won't
mention churches.

When I read your letter about Lesley, I didn't know whether
to cry or scream. Kate, it's too damn much. And just your
style, two handicaps, each one more devastating, a dumb
transvestite, albeit beautiful and sensitive, just so he can split
your heart in pieces.

Have you thought of seeing a psychiatrist, the real thing,
not the test-givers, the counselors, the gurus? Do they even
have the real thing up there? I doubt it. The town would
drive him/her crazy, too. Nobody is exempt, given the right
circumstances. I'm serious.

How can someone who jumped into the sexual fires with
Francis go two years without a date? It's not grief. Don't kid
yourself. Read one of your letters out loud before you send it.
You could construct a bibliography on depression from your
one-liners, from your quotes. Don't you read male writers
anymore or anyone on the continent? Do you remember your
first degree? Or have you lost yourself in library fines and
the *World Book Encyclopedia?*

Poached eggs in a Pyrex coffee pot! Standing up! I wish
I could come up there and pull you out of the mire with a rope.
But the baby is running a fever, and we're broke. Pleasant
Ridge is a long way from the George Washington Bridge,

m'dear, but it ain't all the way to Lapeer.

I talked to my pediatrician about you. It was either him or the butcher. Things are a bit confining without a car. He said: "Anyone your age who has lost all interest in sex and can't sleep is depressed, and just to get clinical, those two symptoms are part of the Big Six, and you have most of them." That means you are VERY depressed. It takes no M.D. to figure that one out, but maybe his credentials will make a difference. You always took all your itches to Dr. Mossman. He died, 46, his wife found him in the library where he went to read a journal after a party. I'm sure he was the last city doctor to make house calls.

Kate, leave town! Write soon, and say something to me. No quotes. No stories about library patrons. Something about you and what you're going to do with the rest of your life. Did Francis ruin you? He loved your spirit (well, your body, too; but he had lots of offers and he chose you), all that talk, all that silence at the right time. He'd turn over in his narrow grave if he could see you now. There, Kate, swallow that.

Forever,
Parker

◢ 6

Nov. 23, 1962

Dear Parker,

One thing you don't know is how scared I am. How I feel when I'm not in the library or my apartment.

I look the way I do on purpose. Other men are not like Francis. I knew that every day I was with him from the beginning to the afternoon I saw him in that hospital bed.

Don't you remember how you hated single life? I've had a few proposals—even looking dowdy, dumpy—whatever word you want to use to describe what I seem to be now. I can be bored by myself.

Maybe I am depressed. But just because I'm alone doesn't mean I've lost my fiery spirit. Tell that to your smarty pants baby doctor!

I'm following your instructions and not quoting anybody. So it is a short letter.

Enclosed is Maurice Sendak's *Really Rosie.* For the baby. She'll grow into it.

I can't compromise. I can't marry an engineer, no offense. You didn't grow up where I did. You are not me. I'm doing the best I can.

You are right. There are no psychiatrists here.

Love,
Kate

◢7

The psychiatrist stood up and sat down. He is not tall. "What brought you here?"

"My life is like a Kafka novel."

"In what way?"

"I see what it is, and it scares me."

"How scared are you?"

"One night I fell asleep with a cigarette in my hand, and the couch caught fire."

"I don't understand."

"Well, I don't smoke, and I can't sleep. So I thought I'd try it for something to do."

"Smoking is an unusual choice for someone with your medical history."

"The point is, I can't sleep; that's why I came in. That, and I have a friend who's a true believer. And she wouldn't let up."

"And you didn't want her to."

"I guess."

"When was the last time things were right?"

"I was twenty-three."

"When did the sleeping problem start?"

"When I was in high school. . . . When I was twenty-three, the man I loved died. He was fifty-six and it was unexpected. But I expected it. I always expect bad things, and they happen. I was lucky to have three years, very lucky. Don't hand me any cheap clichés about a father complex."

"Why are you angry?"

"I don't know."

"Anger is a very effective distraction."

"I broke a set of dishes once. That's real anger."

"When?"

"The day he died, one by one. I never cried."

"Tell me about him."

"He took care of me. Isn't that what men say? 'I'll take care of HER!' He would never have said that. His words were as hand-picked as his clothes. He was never clumsy. That meant a lot to me. He was in charge, so to speak. In bed, he knew where he was going and how to get there. And he had the most wonderful sense of humor. He never told a joke. He was funny. He gave me a lot of advice, and he was gentle. I grew up with explosions. Foul language for supper, and blame. Everybody in my family blamed someone else, and if they ran out, they hit on the Republicans and the Jews. I was ten years old before I knew fish-eyed kike wasn't all one word. What else do you want to know?"

"Did you live together?"

"He came and went."

The doctor handed me the Kleenex box. He ignored the revelation. I did too.

"He read to me in bed. He made me hot toddies. He screwed my brains out. Isn't that what men say now? Screw is not the word. This was long and slow, and not twisted. Before I met him, I made a career out of masturbation!"

The doctor didn't smile. "You are not here to entertain me, Miss McGhee. This nameless man loved you, what else did he do for you?"

"Isn't love enough? He carried me in the shower with my clothes on and taught me how to play."

"Where did you meet him?"

"What possible difference does that make?"

"Everything makes a difference, Miss McGhee. Everything has a reason."

"I met him on a park bench. I was reading a book of haiku. He was resting. He was very good-looking."

"And you, Miss McGhee? What did you look like?"

"What a strange question. Ordinary. I have always been very ordinary-looking."

"Therapy is like school in some ways. A little homework: Why do you want to appear ordinary when you are most extraordinary? And you must, on some level, know it."

I sat down in the chair. He leaned back in his swivel. "If you talk about what we say in the hour, it dilutes the therapy. If you can't hold onto the anxiety until the hour, we can't work with it. It's a tool. Therapy hurts. We will uncover things you never realized were covered up. I want to hear more about this nameless, motherly man."

"Motherly?"

I sat for a full thirty minutes saying nothing. He looked at me the whole time. "Good afternoon, Miss McGhee," he said at last. I could have walked out.

o o o o o

"And we were in bed. I must have been seven or eight. My father smoked Camels. My mother played the piano in the living room: 'White Cliffs of Dover,' 'Lilli Marlene.' Do you remember the words? Ration books. Hoarding. We were in bed, and the fly on his pajamas had some buttons missing. Nothing happened. But the way he held me, just that way, I'm not stupid. I know there are connections; that way, that's how I want to be held after I make love . . ."

"It is not unusual for lovers to embrace after an orgasm."

"You don't understand. It's not an embrace, I am held, he held me tight, because I was terrified, Francis, I mean, because I was terrified, it goes away slowly."

"What goes away?"

"I feel like the walls are breaking down, that something will get me. The boogie man."

"And, now, Miss McGhee, now that he is dead . . ."

"Oh, now? Now I cry."

"You don't tell others about your feelings?"

"There are no others."

"You sleep alone?"

"Yes."

"I want you to take some medicine that will help us. The medicine is a stopgap, but it will calm you down enough for us to get at things."

"I am calm."

"Yes. And what you pay to keep that calm is hard to calculate."

"I'm calm."

"Are you calm at night? Are you calm inside those baggy clothes?"

"I could walk right out of here, you know?"

"I hope you won't."

Five minutes pass. "Is it so awful to want to be held after intercourse? Can this be why you have insulated yourself against men? I doubt it. We are skating on the surface. It's the right ice rink, but the deep, scary stuff is not so easy to pull out."

He handed me the prescription. "Here is my home phone number. If you need to call me, you may. The parking lot is not safe at this time of night. Be sure to ask the guard to walk you to your car."

"I don't drive. Parker is picking me up."

"Good night, Miss McGhee."

* * * * *

"And what else did he do with you?"

"With me? We read together, we talked. After a year, we took walks."

"You waited a year?"

"His wife was a piece of celery. All his money went for nurses, upkeep. It was earmarked. His time. His money. You need time to walk. The second year we were together his business improved, his son got a job. A little more money, a little more time. His son was away at college, so he stayed over a couple of nights a week. He called it a windfall."

"Like apples?"

"Right."

"And you walked with this extra time."

"That's right."

"It sounds like an idyll, Miss McGhee."

"It was an idyll."

"Was it anything else?"

"Well, it grew into an idyll. I thought it was only a convenience at first. For him."

"You didn't trust him?"

"Should I have?"

"I don't know. Who do you trust?"

"Parker."

"Only Parker?"

"That's right. I don't trust myself. If I were on the right track, I wouldn't need you, right?"

"Do you trust me?"

"Of course not. I'm waiting to see what you say. You said this was just the beginning."

"And these walks?"

"They were wonderful. I loved being beside him. He was so sure of himself. I felt safe. I could relax."

"Relaxing is not easy for you?"

"Ha. Ha. Are you making fun of me?"

"Why do you think that?"

"No, it's not easy. And, he was different from everything and everyone. He was all I wanted. Do you have any idea what it's like to wait every day of your life to get away and finally do it and find him? It was everything."

Silence.

"He knew me. I pretended nothing with him, and he was never angry, not really angry, with me."

"Miss McGhee, you are telling me a man with a wife who squeezed his last dime from him with a hopeless illness, whose almost-dead body reminded him of his own age and fate, was never angry? Surely you don't believe what you are saying!"

"He wasn't mean to me, don't you understand? I told him to go away at first. I didn't seek out a married man. He was caught."

"Do you, did you feel caught, too?"

"Of course."

"I mean, before you met him."

"No. I felt free. I got away. By myself. I paid my own way. I'm paying for this, aren't I? Nobody ever gave me anything."

"Perhaps that statement is truer than you want to believe. The hour is over, Miss McGhee. I'll need to change the times for next week . . . I'm going ice fishing."

✿ ✿ ✿ ✿ ✿

Dec. 20, 1962

Dear Parker,

I haven't lost my mind. I'm writing you letters because I don't want to talk to you on the phone. There are all sorts of rules to therapy and I want to keep clean.

I'm afraid if I start talking, I'll spill the beans, as they say.

I have what is called an agitated depression—I pulled that one out of the doctor. He doesn't like labels and jargon, but I had to know.

It ain't easy, but I guess you knew that. Have found a room in a widow's house. My books are in storage. The widow's name is Smith. She's nosy, all the expected things, but I bring her murder mysteries from the library and she thinks I'm an angel— to my face, at least. We share the bath, and it's very cheap. The doctor is not.

I have lost 15 pounds. Ms. Smith is a terrible cook.

Love,

Kate

✿ ✿ ✿ ✿ ✿

Dec. 26, 1962

Dear Kate,
You are crazy. Writing letters in the same city! Okay. I'll keep
within the boundaries. You carry everything to the extreme!
Everything. I'm so glad you're back.
Love,
Parker

o o o o o

Jan. 10, 1963

Dear Parker,
Have a job at the university library, lowest man/woman on
the totem pole, but I'm thrilled . . . They remember me—
the boss, that is. Found the latest French and German writers in
translation and took them all out. It's a splashy beginning.
I still can't sleep, but I feel alive at night.
Love,
Kate

o o o o o

"Hello. This is Dr. Koltonow."

"This is Kate McGhee. I just thought of something. I can't say
it to your face. My mother wore men's clothes. Men's under-
shirts, a man's watch, jockey shorts. What does that make me?
Francis made me forget all that. I never told him. He made me
feel small. He called me a treasure."

"Miss McGhee, I'm not going to hang up on you. Take a
breath, a long breath. Have you got a beer there?"

"Mrs. Smith does."

"Drink it, and try to sleep. I'll see you in the morning at eight,
a cancellation. Can you be late for work?"

"I guess so."

o o o o o

"Tell me more about Francis."

"Francis? I thought you'd go for the childhood stuff. Aren't mothers to blame for everything?"

"Focus, Miss McGhee."

"Why are you so formal?"

"Because you are an adult, not a child. In here, you are not Katie."

"Well, I was Katie to Francis. He tried to call me Katherine, as near as he came to being pompous. But, in bed, I was Katie. I knew who I was then!"

"I'm not so sure."

"What do you mean?"

"Answer my questions, and we'll try to find out."

"Well, he never talked about his wife, he didn't lie to me; he lied plenty to them—so he was a halfhearted liar, I guess. All right, he was a liar. If he lied to me, I believed him. I never questioned what he told me. When I trust somebody, I don't examine their every word . . . he was short, about my height. He wore expensive shoes. He was like me—quiet in public and a real talker when we were alone. I liked that a lot. He was neat, but he liked my apartment. Messy. I only had things I wanted in it. I only invited people I wanted to be there. Sometimes he talked in his sleep. I liked his hands. Soft. He had a habit of pushing my hair out of my face. What else is there to say?"

"You are thinking about Francis. What comes to mind?"

"He drank a little too much. That's the long and short of it. What do you want from me? He was loyal."

"Loyal?"

"Yes. To me. Parker. His wife. No, I guess he had no choice. She was already dead, wasn't she? He was married to a dead woman, and he never talked about it."

"Perhaps he was like most of us, a mixture. But what was there about him of such enormous appeal? That's what we need to look at."

"He let me do as I please. He saved me."

"From what?"

"From everything outside my pink room, outside his bookstore. Everything angry. Everything ugly."

"Like babies and blind dates?"

"Yes."

"From experiment?"

"Yes."

"Do experiments always fail?"

"No, they explode. The chem lab is full of shattered test tubes."

"Tell me about your work."

"All my bosses were corrupt. Some hid it better. They all flew into rages, except the minister. Like my father. Big and little fits. Francis was different. Men like to kick the weakest things around. Maybe the minister did too. But his public face was tolerable. My work is a joke now. But, in the library, people treat me with respect."

"And that's what you felt Francis did, treated you with respect. I think you're right, Miss McGhee, and you earned every bit of it."

o o o o o

"Why do you think your mother played the piano while you lay in bed with your father, all that summer? I'm not going to patronize you. Oedipus means something."

"I don't know."

"Think about it."

"My mother never touched me."

"Your mother was sick, Miss McGhee. I've read the letters you sent me, but you will have to talk about her in the hour. We have time. You have to."

"Sick? Nobody ever thought so before. Nobody said so. What do you mean, sick?"

"I mean gone, gone away. Let's skip the fancy terms. Think

about it. The hour begins and ends just like reality. We have already gone over three minutes. Please leave by this door."

"Why?"

"The next patient wishes to remain anonymous. We're getting someplace, Miss McGhee." And he actually shakes my hand. How far is it from a handshake to a hug?

◢ 8

"Could we take a walk outside?"

"You must have a good reason for breaking the rules. What is going on?"

"I just feel like I can't sit in this chair. Francis's wife died. Finally. I don't know the details. I learned about it after the funeral. His son is a doctor now in Vermont. I stayed out of the bookstore; I don't even know who works there. Who could go back to those rooms and the smells that aren't there?

"The store is mine: the mail-order business, the file drawers. I have meetings with the attorneys in the middle of the day. Just like the movies—long library tables and brass lamps with green glass shades. The Penobscot Building crowd.

"Francis left detailed instructions. His son has to stay out of it, or he won't get the house. According to the man who called me on the phone, everything was planned very carefully, a long time ago. I find it hard, looking back and knowing how death haunted Francis on every corner—his death, her death, death itself."

"Go on."

"I talked about death, too, right in the middle of things. He couldn't reassure me enough. I couldn't get enough reassurance. Once he put my hand in his lap. 'Stop talking,' he said."

"And?"

"I want to mash my face into his chest and scream. I think I remember how to scream. It's done with the mouth open and the back arched, and it comes when you least expect it."

"You think you'll go on screaming and not be able to stop?"

"What do you mean?"

"You choose very controlled friends. Francis was a master at putting the pieces of his life side by side, in spite of the pull of each one. No talk about his life before the accident, his childhood—you could be sure of him, of what he wouldn't say. And Parker? She's as closed-mouthed as you'll ever find. As focused. The library is control. Order. A salute to the alphabet! Your pink room? Only pink. Think about it. And now you do nothing to this room at Mrs. Smith's. Isn't that control too? To do nothing? No compromise. All or nothing!"

"So?"

"What do you wear when your mother wore jockey shorts?"

"I wore nothing. I took off my underpants."

"Only for awhile. Don't be so concrete. I use that as one example. The baggy clothes are not just to hide your body. They are baggy to hide your indecision. Where do you go from Francis?"

"Here. I have you."

"This, Miss McGhee, is a financial arrangement. The hour begins and ends. You work things through. I am talking about a lover. Not a teacher. Here we examine your feelings. Out there, so far, you want them limited, controlled. Without risk."

I am looking at the wall of green and white medical journals. My legs won't move.

◢9

"What do you think?" Seventy dollars a month—a whole house.
The landlord thinks it will be at least a year before the freeway
connects up. The paint is peeling outside, and the porch must be
sidestepped, but the inside is beautiful: two fireplaces and the
windows lock. I don't need good paint, just enough for the duration—and a roller.

So here I am with the radio on and the windows open. Good-
bye, Mrs. Smith. A clean sweep. I bought a mattress and the
landlord left a couch; I covered them both with white sheets.
Parker brought over a reading lamp and a candle: "One can't get
by without the necessities, Kate." I added a wicker basket for
oranges, so I can have breakfast in and cut down on the glare.

"I rented a house I can afford and whitened it up," I keep
telling myself. Parker was sitting here last night, peeling an
orange, with her feet draped over the couch: "These sheets
smell like Clorox. I feel like I'm back home with the diapers!"

◢ 10

Two months went by. I met Sam at the library. He brought in a stack of Saul Bellow, all overdue. He came back two days later and took me out for pizza. I invited him home to see what I'd done with the house. He insisted on touching up the baseboards and I let him. I have never been good with my hands. "Paint the whole thing over, if you want to," I thought, thinking about Bellow's first line: "If I'm going crazy, it's all right with me." Not even Francis had read all of Bellow. But we never got around to talking about the novels. Because as soon as the turpentine was dry on his hands, as soon as the soap took away the smell of the turpentine, he got right down to the physical. And, that's all it was. He never read a real book in his life. Bellow had been for his brother from Chicago.

We made an agreement. A trial period. Things were okay until he was laid off and the recession speeded up: "I'm not sweeping floors," but I think he would have, if any had been available to sweep. Janitors are unionized.

Instead, he sat around and complained about my housekeeping. Plus, he turned into a sex fiend. Sound good? It wasn't. For one thing, all I ever did was close my eyes and imagine he was Francis. It took a leap of imagination because he was so muscular. The candle burned low, and he continued—big and stiff—and lost in his own heat. He ripped off so many bras, I finally went along with the trend and stopped wearing one.

I went to work every morning and came home with a six-pack and a sack of hamburgers. Sam paid the rent with his unemployment check. We went to jazz concerts on Sunday nights on the library lawn, and kept our thoughts to ourselves.

I don't know when I realized I wanted him to leave. I knew I was scared the night he pulled out my diaphragm and threw it against the wall. "I can feel it," he said.

July became August, Parker went to the lake, and there was a water shortage. "They're looking for a chemist at Stroh's," Sam told me soon after. I was shaving my legs with his razor, and he lectured me about private property and grabbed the razor out of my hand.

"Great," I said, "people will always be drinkin' a little beer."

I came home on my lunch hour and threw the sheets and my clothes in a suitcase, shoved my library books in my bag and left. "Let him keep the mattress," I said out loud.

Then I called the landlord from work and told him what I'd done and why. He said the deposit would take care of it, and he'd never let on where I moved. I had the phone disconnected.

I needn't have bothered because Sam didn't even come by the library.

The recession is worse now, and I'm over at Parker's for the rest of the month until I find another bargain. They're around, if you can afford to bide your time.

One thing more. The next man who gets my body gets it at his place on Saturday afternoon. These overnight combats are a real step backwards.

Parker says I sound hard, but Dr. Koltonow sees my point. It's a question of antecedents. What follows Saturday afternoon is Saturday night, dinner out and a good-night kiss. Passion is out of the question.

The reference librarian has a sister whose husband died, and she's renting out her upstairs—one big room—with a tub *and* shower, furnished, plus dinner weeknights, for a hundred dollars and a deposit. She has twin boys, eight years old.

A word on masturbation: It makes things worse. And you're right back where you started—thinking about it all the time. Dr. Koltonow says nothing. He's on to greener pastures, my father.

So I'm left with my hands, and there's nothing more lonely. He says married people do it when their partners are away or sick, and I guess that's supposed to make me feel better. It doesn't.

I bought some birth control pills, just in case. Dr. Koltonow is going to Europe for a month. "Bon voyage," I said. He shook my hand and told me someone was covering his practice. "With a blanket?" I said, and didn't wait for his reply.

On night school: Who's kidding whom? Everyone is there for a pickup. Singles bars are big, too, and discount houses. I'm not drawing any parallels. This is 1963.

Well, I've given up house painting. This attic has wallpaper— too girlish pink-and-blue, but it's good enough, and the bed is soft. What I really like are the window seats. I sit here reading e. e. cummings in the moonlight. Barbizon nightgowns last forever.

◢12

I sold the bookstore and put the money in the bank. It's drawing interest. The attorneys think I'm stupid, but I have no head for investments. Why should I trust them? Sometimes you know what you have to do.

Good night, Francis. I ache for you, standing up, sitting down —even behind your cloud of smoke.

In my dreams, my navy surplus sweater is flying through the air.

Dr. Koltonow just got back from Europe in time to see me laid low with bronchitis. He was noncommittal about the money. Parker brought the lemons this time.

◢13

I don't know what's the matter with me. I can't stop crying. Thank God, it's the weekend. Dr. Koltonow says I only appear worse, but he's not the one mired in a Kleenex box. He said a lot more, but what matters is what he did. He was going to a wedding, and he gave me the number there and said pills wouldn't help at this point, but he'd see me between appointments if I needed him.

He looks tired.

◢14

Work has been hard lately. The younger students are not glad to be there, and they behave badly. I always step back now when a popular book is on hold because I had a spell of grabbers, and one actually hurt my hand.

Since I came here, a man who looks like Sydney Greenstreet has been taking out the new British fiction by women before I get to them myself. Some slow-moving remarks about the coq au vin at the Pontchartrain Wine Cellars or a complaint about the heat, and he's out the electric door.

The saddest patron is an aging redhead who has tried for a Ph.D. in psychology and English. She finished the coursework, but she can't pass the orals. She took out Bowlby, the big three-volume work that just came out, on child development, and *Madame Bovary*, and Sylvia Plath's poems. I've never been able to put all that together until this morning when she told me she had been nominated for the Nobel Prize and turned it down. "Sartre was right, don't you think?" I managed to stamp her out and slip in a bookmark I'd been saving for Parker. It's a quote from A. E. Housman about Mithridates learning to take a little poison at a time. Probably the worst thing I could have done, but I had to leave her with something besides three due dates.

I told Dr. Koltonow and added some disorganized words on all the people who ride the bus and talk to voices; he responded with a cliché. I got up and kicked the footstool as hard as I could. It's an Eames chair, and I know he loves it. Then I left early and cried all the way home. They call it "acting out." There's a name for everything. I don't want to know the name for the redhead. I don't want to know.

◢ 15

The man who looks like Sydney Greenstreet came in today. He appears to be reading Doris Lessing, but he skips around some. Things were slow, and I walked over and asked him what he thought of the old woman who dies with her cat. He looked startled. "I didn't think anything. I cried." He went right back to the printed page. I took a deep breath. Another example of going too far. I couldn't be satisfied with a little light conversation.

◢ 16

The man who looks like Sydney Greenstreet asked me out for dinner. He made it specific—the Wine Cellars, Friday at seven; I'm to meet him there, he will bring me home.

I bought a belt for my black silk jumper and pinned up my hair. I thought about him all afternoon while the reference librarian told me what she'd done for the last three months.

His name is David Broadhead, and he's from the Midlands. We talked all evening without moving from the table. Stout and champagne, Black Velvets, snails and french bread. I picked my way through the chicken and ate an apple dumpling with a pitcher of cream and considered ordering another one. I didn't have the heart to let on cigar smoke bothered me.

The conversation never strayed from London. His family died in the war, but he has been back. I have no idea what he does for a living, but he turns forty next Sunday, and he invited me to come read the *Times* and have birthday cake for breakfast. A proposition, if I ever heard one, and I accepted.

He lives three blocks from the library. His name is not on the mailbox. Maybe he's a secret agent. One thing for sure, he's no cook. The cake came from the bakery. The coffee pot was plugged in right beside me, and three cups gave me the jitters. We read the paper. At least I read all I wanted of the *Book Review*, and he moved along through the rest. Then he brought out a bottle of brandy and two snifters, as if it were what he did every Sunday morning. "Put some ice in mine; I'm no connoisseur." He also turned up the air-conditioner. There is a Vermeer over the couch next to a long gilt-edged mirror. The apartment is a mess, and I love it.

"You have amazing ankles," he said, and he rubbed them while we considered Lessing's beginnings in Rhodesia before she moved to London. I liked the sound of his words. The clasp broke on my barrette, and I got scared. "I've got to get back now," I lied.

"When will I see you again, Katherine?" He hauled himself up off the floor and looked me in the eye for the first time.

"I'm working days this week," I managed.

◢17

Dr. Koltonow has a tan. It is July 1964 and raining hard. You can hear the dentist's drill in the next office.

"So my mother took these men, year after year, into her room. What kind of a man would go in that room?"

"The decor?"

"What decor? The bed was piled high with *Photoplay* and *Modern Screen.* There was only a little space left to sleep. The end of the bed and part of the mattress was sawed off and put in the corner. The shades were pulled, and Kennedy half-dollars rose in piles on her nightstand . . ."

"You are screaming, Miss McGhee."

The drill drones on, and I have to wait to say it: "I'll tell you what the room looked like some other time. Men's clothes are what I can't understand. How can any woman wear men's clothes and do what she did?"

"How do you know about these earlier times?"

"Other women. Neighbors. I know she left every morning ten minutes after my father started up his truck. A neighbor followed her once, and at the bus stop some man picked her up in a car. For years, I believed she went shopping every day. That's what she told me."

I feel sick to my stomach. "What good does it do to talk about this? Do you know what shame feels like?"

"How does it feel to you?"

"It feels . . . it's not what I know . . . it's what I imagine . . . what she did . . . some kind of snobbery on my part . . . the men she picked . . . their hands . . . what they said . . . her men's clothes aren't anything . . . it was her body . . . I can't go on with this."

I look around the room at the studio couch by the window where I never sat and the rain falling. I know what it feels like to be drenched. Is the man who looks like Sydney Greenstreet . . . another motherly man?

"Miss McGhee, I don't know why your mother wore those clothes. I can only guess."

✿ ✿ ✿ ✿ ✿

When I get home, I make a pot of hot chocolate and drink it all. The rain is still falling, and the moon is bright.

◢18

It's Indian Summer, and we went to the drugstore at the Sheraton and ordered hot-fudge sundaes. I bought two *New Yorkers* and was about to suggest reading them on a park bench. "A belated birthday present," I said.

"Maybe this is another afternoon for air-conditioning," David added, taking my hand. I held on tight. His hands were damp as he turned the key in the lock. He lives right next to the Merrill Palmer Institute in one of those dirty brick houses. We walked past the entry and the Vermeer.

"Would you like to prop your feet up, Katherine?" I settled into the chair, and he fixed us ice water. He sat on the couch, and we said a few words about the humidity before we got around to the *New Yorkers*. I flipped through the ads. Nobody has called me Katherine since Francis. I plunged in.

"Your hands are nice. I like soft hands." I unbuttoned my blouse and pretended to read. He walked over and pulled me up. "I wake up at night thinking about you," he whispered. He did not let go.

"Keep talking, Mr. Broadhead."

By the end of the afternoon, we had ruined our clothes and spilled baby oil all over the carpet. "I have no intention of going home looking like this." So we walked into the bedroom and pulled the sheets back. "My breasts are starting to sag." I leaned over the pillow. He laughed. So did I.

I don't know what it is, but I think I found something. We're going to the Pete Seeger concert. They kicked Seeger out of the art museum before he even arrived the last time. The whole town got in on the fight, and he finally showed up at the United

Dairy Workers' Hall. I was there, and I'll be there again this time.

I'm wearing my jumper without the belt and some jewelry I borrowed from Parker. Mexican silver. It makes quite a splash!

I found out what David Broadhead does. A labor lawyer. His cronies walked over to be introduced. One of them was married. They stood around waiting for me to say something, so I waxed forth on Woodie Guthrie's family so as not to disappoint them. I left his sex life alone and skipped the disease. After the sing-along and propaganda, we took a cab back to David's apartment. I propped my feet up and considered my options.

"Stay the weekend, Katherine," his voice was low. "Take off your dress," he advised.

"I could use a little whiskey to relax," I reminded him.

His hands were under my jumper: "You don't want to relax. You want to think about this." His fingers were wet, and he did it all with his hands. "I'm afraid I might crush you," he explained.

"Don't stop," I was too loud.

It's embarrassing, and I told him so. "You're so young. God, Katherine, lay back. Let's hear that scream again!"

And I'm not going anywhere, but right here, in a sweat, saying all those words I thought I'd never say. "We can't stay in this room all weekend," I remind him.

"We can try," he looks up.

And he is in my mouth.

◢ 19

Dr. Koltonow is grinning. "56/40—Not bad, Miss McGhee."

"Are you laughing at me?"

"No, I'm tallying up numbers."

"Then add this. I'll be gone four days, to Toronto."

"Congratulations. Do you feel like an adult?"

"Sometimes."

"Why are you angry? Is your new friend a bad influence?"

"I feel angry all the time. I still hate Sam, and he's gone. I think I hated him from the beginning, and I couldn't tell him, to his face, to go or stay. He wasn't anyone to be afraid of, just ordinary —there were a million Sams on my block. They didn't play tennis or graduate from high school, but they were there grabbing things out of your hands and slamming doors. You make me mad, too. I'd like to scream at the reference librarian—her mouth runs through my head—and I dream about that silly, long-sleeved dress she wears. Cats are tearing out her eyes, and she is dead. Look out the window. It's a hailstorm. I love storms. I love you. I love you, Dr. Koltonow."

He doesn't exactly smile, but he looks as if he understands. "You can wait in the waiting room, if you go out the door and come in again. It's a bad storm. I have another patient who wishes to remain anonymous."

They call this transference. Trust is an old-fashioned word for the same thing. I go out and come in again. The waiting room is empty. My curiosity is aroused. I wonder who is that worried about what other people think. It must be someone with a job, an important job. Someone with a lot to lose.

◢ 20

"I don't know, but I think I've done a lot better."

"You have. The same things are at work, but there's more for you. What do you think is under that weight?"

"Let's see how smart I am. Anger? Rage?"

"Why are you angry now?"

"I'm not looking for a savior. I'm not going to marry him. His rooms will do."

"Does he talk about his job?"

"We talk about what we're reading and once in a while we hit on the city. He went to a boarding school after the war. The only one in his family to rise. He doesn't drink much. He doesn't walk either."

"I see."

"I haven't told him about you. He's enlightened, though. He's read Freud and Freida Fromm Reichman."

"And, he's there."

"Yes, he's there. There are some things I don't want to tell him. There's plenty I don't want to know. The twins cry at night. They keep their windows open, and I sit in the window seat and listen. I wonder who slept in my room before it all fell apart. Maybe it was the guest room."

"Are you sleeping better?"

"I'm sleeping better. Why am I crying?"

"It's time to go back and talk about your mother. This is the hardest part."

"I've decided to make him my landlord. He has an empty flat on Grand Boulevard. Fireplace. Porch. A place for all seasons. Can't pass it up."

◢ 21

"David, come over here. I'm freezing. The pipes don't work. I can't even take a shower."

"How's the electricity?"

"The lights are on, if that means anything."

"Make some coffee, and I'll be there in an hour."

I'm wearing my winter coat when he walks in—packages falling out of his hands, his muffler too tight. "Take off that bloody coat," he says, pulling a quilt out of a Mosley's box. A pale yellow and white miracle. I stand still, my coat tight around me. The next package isn't a package; it's a grocery bag: Cadbury bars, a quart of cream, and raspberry jam. "Why am I in love with a woman who hasn't sense enough to visit a grocery store?" The last package is schnapps. "To clear your sinuses," he says. I know I should have a clean teacup, but I don't. I drink straight from the bottle—sashaying around the room with the quilt around my shoulders, the coat kicked in the corner. What I like about David is he doesn't say a word about spilling. He is too busy unbuttoning his pants.

Two hours go by before he calls the furnace man. "Do you think you can last till five?" he covers the receiver.

"I should be asking *you* that." I am in no hurry to see the furnace man.

I thought better of the weekend in Toronto. I like it, right where it is, three blocks from the library. It's been so long since I felt appreciated.

Lying by his side, I told him: "I hate this city, but behind closed doors, all cities are the same." He is tracing a little blue line in my breast, and I am soft. He is watching my face. I feel like a cat being petted. "Do it to me, for God's sake. And hurry up. Please."

He is bossy, too. "Leave your breasts loose," he says. I put on his pajama bottoms and draw the string. We take time out to sleep. "Do you want to come again?" he offers.

"Yes, as a matter of fact, I do.

"You know, I've spent the better part of my life hungry. I've had another lover, my mother was crazy, not to mention fat and coy. Why should I lie to you? I have a million defects: I'll cost you a fortune in doctor bills. I'm scared of airplanes. I hate parties. I like to talk to one person at a time, and not many altogether, at that. I have a terrible temper, but when anyone else blows up, I die inside. You're a damn fool if you want me. I'm still in love with a dead man."

"Maybe you need lessons in forgetting."

I left out the part about the psychiatrist. I left out the fact that I'm so scared and aroused at once, my teeth ache.

"Katherine, I'll take care of you," was all he said.

He touched my face. "I want to live with you."

"You wouldn't like me all night, every night. I can't sleep. I have a friend, and we ring each other up at odd hours. I read in bed with the lights on. I'm even messier than you. I hate to cook, and you know it. I don't even fix breakfast. I eat an orange and go. You'd expect the usual things, don't kid yourself. What more could I do for you? I'm not going anywhere. I don't see other men. My father's dead, and my mother might as well be. How much of me can you stand? Think about it."

"Katherine, you're not funny. You're not cute. Don't you know what love is? You're so busy being clever, you don't see what's sitting in your face."

"I pass on that one."

"Why does anybody marry?"

"Three reasons: sex, children, or convention. Sometimes all three. Don't you think I've thought about it? You have sex. I won't give you children, and neither of us gives a rip about convention. Can't you have raspberry preserves and my chest without hauling out a diet or a brassiere afterwards? That's what marriage is . . . a diet . . . and a brassiere. You're forty-two years old, and I'm telling you all about romance. It ends with the thin gold band . . . it's late, and my eyes burn. My underwear is all dirty and waiting to be washed. Let's get out of here!"

◢ 22

You can wait too long for things. There's money and time now, but I don't love David. I want what he does with my body. But I don't care what happens to him. I would have done anything for Francis. That's love.

When the weather turns cold like this and the sun goes away, I crawl in bed.

David's picture was in the paper today. Above the baggy brown suit and dusty shoes, he is really quite good-looking. The article had more to say about General Motors than he liked.

I packed a wool jumper and some turtlenecks, and we boarded a plane for San Francisco. I owed it to him. On the plane, I kept thinking of Thursdays at the London Chop House. His cronies are in and out. Their talk is specific and endless: judges and deals, Mr. Bluestone, pistols—when and where—and opinion is divided. I could choke on the smoke. "Let's have the mousse, Katherine." It's apple pie for the others. Walter Reuther lives in Rochester now behind an electric fence. They say he builds furniture.

"If you buy a gun, I'm leaving you." He knows I mean it. There's no place to go, and my dreams are killing me.

◢ 23

"You bloody well do whatever you like, when you come right down to it. . . ." David's stomach meets the tablecloth.

"How do you mean?" I could tell he was really mad.

"You're too congested to come to dinner; but you manage a fast recovery and join everybody just as dessert is cleared. You've told me often enough how much you hate shop talk. I guess Joplin stomps her way through any notion of us."

"Us? You are the ABA, huh, David?"

I leave the dinner table with the others, remembering my inhaler—steaming my chest red in the shower, two extra pills, a pot of scalding coffee bribed from room service—and the whole thing makes me jittery enough to commit murder. David doesn't know cigars bother me, and we are off for the concert where there is enough smoke to put me right back where I started.

In the cab, I imagine taking a train back to Detroit, leaving him flat; he's a better landlord than lover.

The club is packed. The opening act hurts my ears, so I disappear fast to the bathroom for one last puff on my inhaler. A young singer named Janis Joplin is a flash. David hates her. But he is too polite to admit it. There's a coarseness about her person, her complexion, her nose. I think it's this—the visuals—that bothers him, a physical thing. It can't be her language. The ABA delegates swear like stevedores. Anyway, you can feel his mind adding up the parts he doesn't like for later.

Janis Joplin is right on the edge; and I'm with her. I act as straight as David; but I know she's not long for this world; and she's hungry for something she's running in the opposite direction from. It's not satin sleeves or sour mash whiskey, and it's not comfort.

Harvey, the attorney from Savannah, makes his big white handkerchief available and acts as if my coughing fits are endearing. You can't help but love Southern manners. At least, I can't. They feel warm, even when they're not. Harvey is an aristocrat, but he tries his best to fit in.

What am I? The more I learn about unions, the more I feel stuffed shirts and stuffed bellies and unending clichés and provinciality just moved to a different address, leaving Grosse Pointe behind, and sit now in stripped-down Chevies on sloping driveways and treeless streets.

David wears his pajama tops and bottoms when we get back to the room. I know better than to get near him. The windows are open, and it's chilly. I can't breathe, lying flat; so I doze off in the chair. Joplin's whiskey voice and cackle trail off into a dream where she is crying, the acne scars gone; but her face bigger, lopsided, and pink. I wake up with a start. The only thing left to read is the Gideon Bible. So I write a letter to Parker on the hotel stationery.

November 1965

Dear Parker,
The labor lawyers hang together. Wretched people. S.F. is wonderful, but I can't wait to get away from this crew. They brag and gossip and they are intimidated by David. He is a nasty person when you cross him.

I can't get enough of San Francisco—the air, the bus rides (with the windows open), and the buildings. The apartments are every sort of pastel, and they all have big bay windows. Art is everywhere. Books, too. Stuffed my suitcase with glossy paperbacks and bought a seascape with a thin frame. You'll love it. The people are from all over the world; and nobody talks about cars.

Heard someone called Janis Joplin tonight. She blistered the smoke, if that's possible, and blistered David, who never said a word, but went into his stiff-upper-lip routine. We are barely speaking.

North Beach is dingy and predictable. The Beats look beat, and cops are everywhere, harrassing. The women are pale and sexless and affect the dancers' neutrality without their sinewy bodies. They wear black tights and dirty dresses. City Lights is another story. It has everything and stays open till 3 A.M.

Had lunch at Tadich's Grill—very uptown. The waiters carry white cloth napkins over their arms; and you don't want to know how good the drinks are. 1849 on the window—all understatement. The steak made me forget David for a minute.

I want to take the train home; but I know I won't. I'm a coward.

Love,
Kate

P.S. Hipsters are different from Beats. They are cool, urbane and funny: "What's shakin', baby?" Harvey, the attorney from Savannah, tells me Lenny Bruce is the one to watch—if I have the stomach for it. You wouldn't catch me too near either one; but I don't mind watching. What about you?

I'll call,
Kate

▲ 24

November 1965

Dear Parker,
This hotel stationery will have to do again. Haven't the energy to
hunt postcards. David is not keen on walking, his words,
so we take cable cars. They are old and ratty; and wide open
on two sides. Called Dr. Koltonow, in tears; and he—of course—
connects the cable cars to my mother. Where are my
boundaries? Where does the track end? The unconscious is
a strong pull; once you accept the fact that it's there, you can't go
back. You must dig out its confusing little bypaths and black
corners. Even here, in this fancy hotel room, my brains are
bursting through my skull.

We, I mean me. The only we today are the room service
waiters, all Orientals, and unusually tall with teeth like squirrels.
We go dancing tonight; we made up and decided on something
slower, sans smoke. I am using a travel iron on my old black
silk.

I'm also rereading *To the Lighthouse*. The mother is all;
Parker, all; and the passages where the seeker goes to the
beach to question the meaning of life and finds no answer—
it's better than poetry. The structure of this book, the language,
never fails me. I read for solace—no high flown discoverer,
me; just a single woman, rubbing up against the beauty of
her words. "Virginia Woolf died with a stone in her pocket,
that exquisite face, like a skull. The bombs were dropping,"
David says, the same bombs that killed his family. Hitler was
keeping his promise; and Virginia thought England was finished.
Leonard Woolf was a socialist; David can't get enough of him.
"Virginia," he says, "is a bit too precious."

There's not a drop of sex, anywhere, in her books. We can
leave that to D. H. Lawrence, can't we? A savior. All that stuff
about the phallus—he doesn't bear rereading. So long ago,
before I even met Francis. Lawrence invented that gamekeeper.

Just knowing you're home with the baby makes me feel better. Books to follow. More monsters by Sendak, *Wild Things* . . . don't worry about her psyche. It's okay to play around with demons in print!

Is there a life of the mind that goes anywhere? MINE CHASES ITSELF IN CIRCLES. I'm having a Cutty Sark early today—I found two tiny bottles from the airplane in my bag. Also, a nap. I must be prepared for a bit of night life. See how those Britishisms slip in on you!

Lenny Bruce is the big gun now, not just with Harvey. "Social satire," they say. But I think these men revel in his crazy rage/an art form/and some real scary stuff. Once you lift the lid and let those words out, whew!

This is a young crowd. Only one Detroit attorney is married, and he might as well not be. He is hanging out with a Chinese whore, and he takes her everywhere. She is not smart. Sorry, Parker, she doesn't have a heart of gold, either. But the other men are titillated, and one told me Dashiell Hammett had similar tastes. As if I cared!

Hammett is Lillian Hellman's lover. This comes word-of-mouth from Harvey. David is the hatchet man in the office; and Harvey is the conciliator. What does that make me? A tag-along librarian who'd rather be in the stacks!

Am trying to enjoy little flecks of pleasure before the wind blows them away.

Love to all,
Kate

▲ **25**

Kate—
You *are* a fool. I'm not saying David is a prize. But he's kind.
Everybody gets mad. I'm mad all the time since I quit drinking.
   How can he know how sick you are when you cover it up
and sit there like a ninny? I think you should apologize for
being a bitch. Tell him you'll still rent the flat, at least. It's
substantial, on the bus line—a deal. How many times have you
moved in the last year?
   It wouldn't hurt you to be bored once in awhile. Do you
think motherhood is paradise at the sandbox? My dryer is
broken. Come on over, Kate, and you can hang the clothes
while I straighten out your life. I'll give you cut rates!
   Kate, he loves you. Who cares about the rest?
                                        Parker

◢ 26

David has little rituals; the way he puts on his slippers, his desk, dusted and organized; I know better than to touch a single pen. I write notes to Parker while he sleeps. Parker is no good on the phone now; she is wiped out at night and too busy in the day. So David has his desk, and I have my bag, ready to pick up and go— or stay. Flexible.

His life is private; and I want to keep it that way. I am talking to Dr. Koltonow. The last patient used up all the Kleenex and threw it on the floor.

"He could have had men for all I care. He is the curious one."

"In what way?"

"There's something he hides. Francis hid all the misery, his wife's beauty, plenty. What was left was pure; this man is tainted. He can't buy me with quilts that cost more than a week in the Caribbean."

"Is he trying to buy you? What does he pay? You pay rent. You walk to work. You pay me. Your sweater is full of moth holes. What the hell has he bought you? A pair of stockings and a quilt? A jar of jam?" Dr. Koltonow throws his pen across the desk. It is not a ballpoint.

"Psychiastrists don't throw things. Where are your rules?"

"You are maddening, Miss McGhee. But you have gone beyond a vaporizer and lemons." He picks up his pen and puts it in a drawer. He puts his feet on the footstool, and we go on.

"What is wrong with being independent? Some things must be done in excess, or they're not real."

"Was your mother independent?"

"She could have been. She had my father's business in her

name, as well as the house. It was a gimmick, a ploy, but it became her threat. She could have left. She wasn't helpless."

"She was crazy. You try to forget that. She was already gone. She locked her bedroom door and lived in the dust, if you'll allow me a metaphor. With her costumes."

"And her men."

"Miss McGhee, does your head shake like that often?"

"My head . . . sometimes."

"When?"

"When a patron grabs a book out of my hand. When David starts in on me."

"Starts in?"

"He thinks he can talk me into marrying him; and he's going to end up out my door. . . ."

"And?"

"And I don't want to be alone. And I don't want to move again. And how could I rent from him and leave him? How do I stop my head from shaking?"

"It's your way of saying 'no.' You have so few ways of saying 'no,' can you afford to cut one out?"

◢ 27

We are sitting in Parker's living room rolling a chime ball across the carpet. She is wearing her leotard and sweating because of it. *The Maltese Falcon* and the brown paper it was wrapped in wait on an end table.

"The more I see of these union men, the more I fear we've traded one set of bastards for another. The reason Walter Reuther stands out as a prince is all the riffraff in the other unions. The question is not: 'Why aren't there more like him?' but: 'How did he manage to get to the top in the first place?' "

"Anyway, Parker, San Francisco was better than anybody told me it would be. Now what?"

"Another baby, m'dear!"

So I fell asleep and took a look at my dreams. They were frightening; but in them babies were smiling and warm, like Parker. Now, on Saturday mornings, I take a crochet class from a woman who lives up the street in a duplex with aluminum siding. She has a little boy who watches us.

I bought some thick needles and got started on an afghan for Parker. The blue yarn falls to the floor every night; and I tell David I'll get prepared for a civil ceremony, if he is serious about marriage. Parker is thrilled.

David plays poker on Friday nights with Jerry and Harvey at Harvey's apartment downtown. David flew out of here with the news and without his wallet. They all called from the poker game to wish me well, and to say they were issuing David IOU's because he had lost his touch as well as his money. I laughed and kept on with the crochet hook and thought about my grandmother and about David and wished he'd come home early and hold my head in his lap under the Vermeer. I think I'll crochet an afghan for us, too. The popcorn stitch goes fast.

◢ 28

Whose idea was it to see Lenny Bruce? We both talked about him: the Hipster over the Beat.

Rumors fly. "Bruce hangs out with musicians. Billie Holiday all over again. Once they nail your ass for dope, you're through!" Parker falls asleep after that piece of exaggeration. How can anyone so cynical believe in a happy ending for me?

We are on the night train to New York City; and I am dozing off. Only the porter is fully awake. Francis rode this train for five years, and he looked forward to what he liked best: intense spurts of bookishness from an unexpected source. The porter grew up in Springfield, Massachusetts—part of the only black family in town; and they all hung around the library. His name is John Bates, and his hair is white.

They're taking away this service. This may be my first and last train ride. It seems only right to bring along a gift. John Bates has read so much it's hard to choose, but Bellow seems right. I inscribe the novel with a reference to Francis. Bates shakes my hand and looks away—a compact man with piano player's fingers—distanced.

"I used to be on the Chicago run. Did you know that?"

"No." I'm about to mention Baldwin's essays, but I think better of it. "Have you met Bellow in person, then?"

"His picture is all. He looks something like Francis. Same size. Three-piece suits."

Mr. Bates shakes my hand again, hard: "I stopped by the shop before they tore it down. I only saw him a few more times after that."

Whatever we want to say about Bellow, Francis and ourselves, we can't say here. Repositories of unspoken sentences, educated beyond our jobs—the library and the train—we wonder together when, exactly, the sun will come up.

When we finally walk in the Blue Angel, early, the crowd is already edgy. A few football stars and their blond girlfriends are sitting ringside. The warmup is a bore. I keep thinking about the porter and Francis. The dark stage, the spot, and then—Lenny Bruce. His pants fit; his eyes tell a lot, too. Parker and I are too absorbed in the spritz to talk until intermission. I speak first: "There's not much that comes my way better than a book; and he's it!"

"He is a book. A book on fire. Burning alive. He pulverizes everything I hate." The other people wait to laugh; but Parker and I are not in our hometown; and we die laughing. "Where does all that rage come from?" Parker is reading biographies now; and sometimes she is too much.

I don't want to know. David was right. Bruce will need more than one lawyer. Parker doesn't say much else, but she wants to go again tomorrow. I pretend to argue, but it's a fine idea. When I find something I like, I keep with it. So here we are again. I'm high on Tedrol, and the smoke is killing me. Bruce is a capsule of darts. We go from the club to the Plaza—the courtyard with the violins. The air is better, and we can talk.

"He'll be coming to Detroit."

"It'll be something to look forward to."

Then we catch *Hiroshima, Mon Amour* at that little theater across from the fountain at the Plaza. Are we glutted on pleasure? Not us. We eat ice cream in bed with fudge that drips all over the sheets.

How can I tell you about that movie? Parker and I strolled through the lights in the little lobby on into the dark and sat down in the invisible steam. I've never seen bodies stretched across the screen like that. Two exiles: a Japanese man and a German woman. I loved their grainy gray images. I loved what they said. I wanted to be lifted into the movie and absorbed in their celluloid lives in that land of whispered secrets.

The twin beds here at the Plaza are soft, the sheets stiff. Parker falls asleep first. She snores. There are no other sounds, not even a dripping faucet.

◢ 29

The little orange bar of Neutrogena slides and melts before my eyes, so expensive, and I am lost in its smell.

David holds the Conair, and I close my eyes. Soon the swirling hair and soapy smell take me away from him. I can't help but wonder where he learned this trick. David has hinted, more than once, he would enjoy a scenario of my lovers' gestures, and words, and more. Each time it happens, I leave early and try to steam away the tawdry idea in my shower.

◦ ◦ ◦ ◦ ◦

Dr. Koltonow is listening. "Go on."

"There's no place to go. I feel I'd be a fool to expect more."

"You can never argue. Only leave. Your anger is killing you."

"He eats ice cream by the quart. For breakfast, mind you. Why does it bother me so much?"

"What is ice cream made of?"

"Who's the comedian now?"

"We must talk about your mother, Miss McGhee."

"I called your house last night. You were out. It was storming. Your daughter was frightened. 'The rain is not always like this,' I told your daughter. I promised her I'd type up the cummings poem: 'nobody, not even the rain, has such small hands. . . .' Is that all right?"

"No, it is not all right."

"Why not? Do you think a patient can damage your daughter?"

"I'm not worried about my daughter. It would break your heart."

"Here we go again." The Kleenex is never far away.

"Back, Miss McGhee, to your mother."

"I dream of drowning in baby oil, the slime covering my eyelids!"

◢ 30

What is true? Not chronology. Facts.

Fact one: My mother bedded down with other men. Most were garage mechanics. The first one I discovered was poor. His son was in my high-school graduating class. He sat alone and failed. I saw his mother once standing in a faded housedress in her garage next to a car with the wheels off.

The second man owned a gas station. His British wife hac. the brains and ambition. They were childless. She gave me a $1.39 plastic clothes bag for graduation and invited me to tea where she sliced one lemon, laid out four sugar cubes, and asked me questions I didn't answer.

The third man was different. He was a genius with a sixth-grade education who never smiled. He taught engineering at a college; all the rules had been lifted to let him in. His wife went crazy one summer afternoon when the temperature reached 90 degrees. She cut paper babies, not dolls, out of a quilt in the front yard. Since a quilt is not paper, and babies are not dolls, there was no doubt about where she belonged.

My mother belonged nowhere; but she stayed in the house. All her men had dirty fingernails: ragged, with black grease, too embedded for Lava soap to reach; and they were all my father's friends. Friendship is complicated, and so is the truth. But these are facts and when I could no longer hide from them, they raced through my head—like a lawnmower gone berserk.

What scared me was the image of those fingernails and where they might go and what they could touch. My mother washed roast beef and lettuce with Ivory soap. She spent hours chasing green flies with a swatter; and she cautioned me to wash my hands before and after I went to the toilet.

If these men entered my mother's secret life, where did I belong and what did they think of me? I spent my adolescence racing from activity to activity, running the school, and staying out of anybody's bed but my own—where I sweated and dreamed of pleasures described in novels I kept hidden under my mattress.

I am the farthest from a liberated woman as you will ever find —tied to dreams of my mother's fat pink body and those greasy men searching for release from their dirty work and lonely wives in my mother's bedroom, locked tight and full of dust and frayed lampcords. Piled high with movie magazines and half-eaten boxes of candy.

How do I tell this to a psychiatrist? How do I say I felt soiled and spoiled before I knew what the words meant?

◢ 31

The wedding plans, such as they are, are set. David finds this a good time for criticism. To make me perfect for the marriage, I guess.

"You live a vicarious life, Katherine."

I am absorbed in the yarn. It has a beginning, middle, and end.

"We are twins," I say. The tears are in my throat.

"I need you," he adds. This is an apology.

I don't know how it happened. One minute I had the hook in my hand and the stitches were predictable. The next, I was ripping out the rows. The wool came from Maine, and it took three weeks before the delivery boy unloaded the boxes. I reached for the scissors and stopped.

"You're all the life I can stand, David. If you don't like walls, get another woman. There're plenty of screamers out there. Women behave like rabbits these days. Get away from me, you bastard!"

But I am clamping and digging into his soft shoulders and if he left, my imprint would be there.

◢ 32

Two days before the wedding David and I were fighting over everything. Edgy, irritable, I let his words get to me. Then he had to fly to Grand Rapids. "What has Gerald Ford got to do with this?"

"Nothing. Why?"

"Who else lives there?"

I was mad when he left and devastated when he got back. He was supposed to meet me at the Chop House; instead the waiter brought a phone to the table: "Two more days to this stint, Kate. There's nothing I can do."

Harvey was sitting alone at the next table. I think he had been stood up; but he carried it off as if neither of us were mad about being there. When I told him about David being away right up to the zero hour, he offered to take me home and spring for lunch the next day at the Sheraton. "It's your last chance," he warned.

It was Friday; so I got there early, walking over from the library. Harvey was already at a table in the back, reading a *Free Press.* I can't blame what happened on champagne, because it was no celebration. We had a pitcher of martinis. I ordered it and I poured, but I can't blame myself. It was being left. It was Friday afternoon. There's something about the end of the work-week in this factory town that's hard to explain but is there anyway.

We got falling down drunk; and Harvey told me David was a fag.

Harvey rented a room right in the middle of the day; and I called my boss with some trumped-up excuse. I can't remember the call; my boss told me about it. I don't think Harvey planned any of it. We couldn't walk, so the room seemed like the answer, at the time. To take an elevator up, where he could explain.

He was in no condition to do anything but talk; and I thought if I just kept asking questions I could make sense of the facts and know what to do with them.

They spilled out: run-on sentences delivered courtroom-style, cold. Without a single breath, Harvey changed the course of my life and made me feel like my mother's daughter. Why should I feel ruined, when I was the one betrayed? I shuddered to think of the times David Broadhead had made me climax with his hands—of the times I had taken him in my mouth. What is homosexuality? Can it be fixed?

After that bombshell, Harvey continued: "Only two of us know, and we don't talk about it."

"Who?"

"Jerry and me. You know how Jerry looks up to him . . . I don't want you to hear the details."

"Harvey, you've made a mistake. You don't understand English boarding schools. All the barristers in London would be fags by some standards."

"Do you have to say f-a-g?"

"My life isn't a courtroom. You've already jumped the fence and dragged me to the keyhole. I'll use any language I like!"

"All right. It was the ABA last year. In the hotel. He hired a whore. A man. I saw him coming out of David's room. He winked at me. He did everything but count the money in the hall. It was a fluke. Five A.M. I was in bad shape myself. Since then, I've thought about things and watched him. Ask Jerry, yourself. I'm only telling you what I saw—not what I heard. The man can't help himself. But he can help marrying you!"

I am picking off my nail polish. The pink flakes pile up in the ashtray. I shove my napkin in the soufflé; bread crumbs are all over the tablecloth. The waiter is watching us.

"Harvey, see if you can get me another drink." I'm on my way to the bathroom. All I do is pee. My mother's warnings about germs are lost; and my silver barrette is hanging from my hair. I shove it in my bag and go back to the table. Harvey must have booked the room by then. I would have done it, if he hadn't.

"I'm not going home. He even owns that."

"He's out of town, for Christ's sake!"

"I see a shrink twice a week. Not an analyst. It's not fun. I live in fear someone might slip, and it would go on my work record. I know a girl who couldn't get into the college of ed because of an episode in the dorm. I lie about it on anything printed. Parker is the only one who knows. Now, you know. Don't ever tell anyone . . . please. I can't risk this job."

By the time we get to the room, I am calm. "Leave him. He'll know. He knows. He can't change. You'll add delusions to your problems, if you think he will!"

"He always did it with his hands; and I liked it. What does that make me? Why did he pick me in the first place? You don't know the half of it. What do you know?"

"I know damn well you better stop screaming, or you'll have the house dick in here; and I know you shouldn't be left alone. And I know I'm drunk. There's not much else to know." Harvey pushed me forward, and we land in bed.

"I'd like to screw you senseless, but I'm not USING MY HANDS! And I can't use anything else right now." I giggle and start to laugh and can't stop. Someone bangs on the wall; and Harvey actually slaps me, hard. Then he holds me. "I had to . . ." he says.

With a dripping cold washrag on my forehead and his fingers tracing the edges of my lips, I finally stop making noise. There is no doubt he has taken charge: "You're sending a telegram to David as soon as we sober up. Put it in print."

I feel spoiled and hopeless and ravenous. "What's wrong with your hands—once?" Harvey wastes no time. A direct invitation clears the air.

"Don't stop . . . maybe you're a fag, too. . . ." He must know my life is smashed; for he rubs slow and on and on. . . . "Let go, Kate." But it takes a long time. And when I come and that little moment, when you forget all the bad things, is over, he tears my dress right down to the hem and grabs me in a death grip against his shirt and pants. His tie is still knotted. That seems like a pretty odd thing to do; but I guess he isn't thinking much about the future; so I don't either.

When it was over, it was all business. And enough of it to occupy us because I understand so little. The facts cleared the way and David denied nothing. He called me every day; and we ate take-outs at night on my porch. Before he left for the coast and realized grapes and lettuce were not much improvement over automobiles, before he got lost in gnarled vines and pale green worms, he sold me the house on Grand Boulevard. We settled on a fair price. I didn't tell him where I got the money, and he didn't ask. I paid cash. I have my own logic. When you drain sex off the top, something is left. Fair play, in this case. And despair.

At first I thought I might cry forever in Harvey's lap; but I sobered up and increased my appointments to three a week, finishing off my savings and leaving no money for remodeling.

The afternoon with Harvey at the Sheraton felt like settling into my mother's lap; and it scared me to death. I still talk to him on the phone and he mailed me a list of contractors; but I rented out the upstairs flat with no help. A thumbtack and a 3 x 5 card on the bulletin board at the library. The first caller was Herr Beil, a German professor who uses a cane and takes my word that there will be renovations within the year. He signed a lease and paid two months in advance. We ride the bus together in the mornings. My finances are in better shape than my life.

Dr. Koltonow hasn't changed. "I bought a vibrator, and it doesn't work." His face is stone. "Are we back to sit-down comedy, Miss McGhee?"

"No, I'm serious. It was too embarrassing to return. Well, at least I didn't marry a fag!"

"Will it hurt less if you call him names?" Dr. Koltonow has a cold and his eyes are bloodshot. "I ignored the signs as much as you did; but they were there. Mr. Broadhead made a desperate attempt at an ordinary life. Was he a bastard?"

I don't have to talk in this room. I pay my bill. I am free to think while the minutes tick by. I can't say what I'm thinking.

"Miss McGhee, we are back to control. Men must have it when you feel you don't. What is the price?"

"I didn't love him."

"I think you did. Love is rarely an idyll. Do you know a novel with more than one grand passion? Francis is dead."

"You're mean."

"All or nothing. Black or white. Reality is what we see in this room. And it is far more complicated."

"Well, Harvey won't get me in bed again!"

"Do you feel you were a bad girl at the Sheraton?"

"You make me sick."

"Answer the question."

"Yes."

"Harvey told you the truth. He seduced you. You let yourself be comforted. How old are you, Miss McGhee?"

"You know how old I am."

"Do *you* know?"

PART THREE

In Spite of Everything

◢ 1

Dear Parker,

Enough postcards. I keep them in the bathroom across from the commode—photo side forward. How about a real letter? I hear Dayan's daughter writes novels, and he is a womanizer! Are the novels any good?

Your girls sound organized. Isn't Rebecca a little young for nursery school? How does a nonbeliever like you make friends in Israel? Tell me if you have quit reading the experts and gone back to literature.

Just remember, I never cared much about vegetation, so don't describe the flowers or the decorations. Tell Ben I think he did a brave thing, the only thing, to move back. This city does not improve.

Dr. Koltonow has encouraged me to get out of the house on weekends, so I have found a group of high-school dropouts who meet Saturday mornings at the branch library near my apartment. They are all working now, and they quit school for different reasons. Four girls and two boys. I'm trying to do something for them and myself. We are writing about the city first; the personal is too scary for me—right now. Journals. Of course, we read, too.

We have begun with black men—Wright, Ellison, and Baldwin, but we plan to see a play by a woman at the Studio Theatre at Wayne this weekend. It's so popular we had to settle for a Sunday matinee. The play is *Raisin in the Sun.* I think it's chutzpah for a white woman to be teaching this class, but we all know I have more than my share of brass. We talk about my limitations and their jobs and Motown (it's in an old house about eight blocks from the branch and ten from my house), and that silly cannon in front of Northwestern High School. The topic that cut the ice is the police; they all have stories about them. We are easing our way into the books. Ellison may be a little too surreal for some, but the oldest

boy/man has the brains for it as well as the experience—
The Invisible Man.

It beats staying in my bathrobe until Sunday night. As long as I'm up, I buy my oranges on the way home and eat lunch out, alone.

Lenny Bruce died. Remember when we heard him in New York? Well, his court battles are over now. My mother died too. A cerebral hemorrhage. You don't want to know about that, and I don't want to tell you. Cremation doesn't burn off the horror, and it's still expensive.

The nearest thing to a social life I have are Sunday night suppers, pot luck, here at the apartment. I provide the whiskey and ice and light the candles. The junior staff comes. We usually have ten people, different ones each week. Book talk, gossip, worries. Herr Beil comes down with his schnapps and leaves with it as well.

June Christie was at Baker's Keyboard Lounge this weekend. I buy my firewood from a stooped-over woman next door. All cut and split and bundled. I haven't had a date in six months.

Don't forget me.

Love,
Kate

◢ 2

You can avoid her body on the cheap satin pillow and the twelve choices of caskets. You can pay to have her burned, and it includes twenty dollars for the obituary. Nobody forces you to have a preacher tell you the Lord is your shepherd. But you can't avoid flowers and phone calls. People you know pay no attention to requests for charitable donations. White gladiolas and blood red snapdragons. Baby's breath. They arrive at the door with a long list of broken families on each card. The delivery man is gaunt, and his steps are carefully plotted.

You dream of catching a train to a country where the alphabet is unrecognizable and the temperature freezes your soul, but you remain in your living room with your bare feet on the coffee table. There's no way to push back your rage and memories.

You might be able to take gin in a teacup, fast, but there's no way you can forget old age and the fact that you will die, too. Parker is in Israel and Francis is dead and Harvey moved back to Savannah. David lisps and lies beside a different boy every night in San Francisco. You feel lonely and lost and sorry you were cruel enough to force him out of your life.

You can stuff the flowers in plastic bags and risk your life getting them to the alley in the middle of the night, but death is real and a plastic bag won't hold it. Even if your mother's corpse has been eaten by fire and her lovers are dead, she is still part of your flesh. You might as well think about the year she sent you to live with your grandmother because you are too exhausted and drunk to do anything else.

Still, after years of therapy's dredging, connecting, crying, hating, blaming, and forgiving, my childhood memories find me in the night, wait for me in gas stations while an unexpected leak in my bicycle tire is fixed. Without a book to save me, where the mechanic's blackened fingernails smudge my credit card, lulled by the predictable revolutions of the dirty fan, I am caught again.

I am seven years old. School is out for the summer, and I sit on the splintered teeter-totter, watching the school buses leave for the long ride to farms between Lancaster and Circleville, Ohio. On her way to the running board, a reckless girl throws her copy of *Wonder Woman* in my lap—the first piece of reading material I owned—the first piece, other than Michigan newspapers— that found its way into my grandmother's house.

One by one, the buses turned onto the four-lane, leaving me brushing dust off my long cotton stockings. I got up, looked both ways, and ran across the highway, down the dirt road—my comic book and schoolbag in the same hand, past the elderberry bushes, through the Queen Anne's lace, down the hill to the place where a cement slab signaled the path to the railroad tracks. Past the tall weeds, I flew over the six tracks and stumbled up the other embankment, not stopping until I stood on my grandmother's front porch.

The heat and the flies and my punishment for being late did not matter; I read the book again and again, hid it, taped it, covered it with brown grocery-sack binding, and had no doubt it would endure. That afternoon I took it with me to the outhouse, where a black and yellow spider hung in midair. I was afraid to kill it, or move the web, for fear it would swing over to my uncovered bottom or shoot up my leg. So, with one eye on the spider and the other on the inky blue hair of Wonder Woman, I sat alone, alert to danger, reading, until I was called to pump water from the cistern.

I did my duties willingly: crossing the track to the post office after school, buying a quart of milk and adding the other groceries, a few each day, to sit on the windowsill or the coolest part of the table. I was the messenger to town because my grandmother (Nana) could not leave her own mother alone. Without me to fetch and carry (so they told me), my great grandmother would go to the county home, and Nana, a penniless widow, would come to live with us in Michigan. My mother hated Nana. She was pretentious; she had no common sense; she spent money on the wrong things. She had doomed my mother to a life with crooked teeth and my father, whom she married at twenty-five to escape Nana. He was her first and last date. She hated Nana, too, for unspoken things that made my mother's face red and her hands shake; and, besides, she told me, Ohio schools were better.

So, one day, as my mother sat picking dead lice out of my head and wiping the dripping kerosene on a towel, I was told of my life in Ohio: "You must study hard, and never, never be late; there is no phone and Nana couldn't leave the house to look for you. You can't have friends over. It would make Nana nervous. She has enough watching to do. You'll learn a lot," she added. "And never, never leave your wraps in the cloakroom; keep all your things at your desk, and this (she pushed her knuckle against my scalp) won't happen again." Rigid, I listened to the sound of the scissors clipping my dripping hair. "You're lucky Nana can do French braids . . . when it grows out . . ."

The next morning I was on a Greyhound bus watching the flat Ohio fields pass by: alfalfa, corn, cabbage—beautiful in varying greens. I tried hard to be a good girl.

My great grandmother was senile. She pooped in unexpected places. Sometimes in my doll's bed; once on the kitchen floor;

often by the front door. I hated her then, and I hate old people now. No amount of logic has made right being alone in that unpainted house with a crazy woman who might burn it down at any unwatched minute, who could be counted on to smear shit at least once a day, who looked evil (sausage curls, thin lips, and penetrating black eyes), not pitiful and weak. She was tall and strong—her hands like clamps.

Winter nights, I fell asleep, next to wrapped bricks, under patchwork, woolen comforters, wondering if Lucretia would rise and kill us. Nana's nightly prayer: "If I die before I wake..." spoke to me. Already I doubted the Lord and could not imagine what a soul was, but that prayer made perfect sense. Would she kill me in the dark with her bulbous, blue-veined hands? Or, on the way to the slop jar, early one morning, would she cover my face with a pillow? When, at last, she tried to, Nana tied her to the bed each night, and her moans and curses signaled safety to me and I slept like a baby in spite of the noise.

Maybe, if I wore my clothes under my nightgown, I could run away before morning, bust loose like Wonder Woman with her inky blue hair and perfect body. Four years later, home in Michigan, I still slept fully dressed. No amount of reasoning stopped me until finally my father used a razor strap on my backside.

Getting sick freed me. Undernourished (Nana saved the money my mother sent for food, and we lived on Lucretia's pension check), weak from three bouts of pneumonia, I rode the Greyhound bus back to Detroit. Lucretia went to the county home. They came for her in a truck—four men. She pushed one into the honeysuckle vines, but the other three were able to buckle her legs to the stretcher. I sat, rigid, on the porch swing. My mother stood by the door. Inside, Nana was busy signing papers. Not one of us shed a tear.

◢ 4

June 5, 1967

Dear Parker,

Met the actor backstage who plays Walter Lee in *Raisin in the Sun*. He's tall and dark and has an Indian nose and he thinks he's funny. His name is Raymon Black and he greets his admirers with his arm outstretched: "I'm black, man . . ."

Next week, we're doing our own version of the play on tape, and he's coming to the library to talk to us.

The journals are moving along, but I'm skittish with this group. I told them *Black Boy* was worth buying, but Richard Wright's fiction was the worst kind of melodrama and they just looked at me. They were more interested in the details of Wright and Baldwin living in Paris. Tidbits about Wright's Parisian wife and Baldwin's homosexuality. Do you remember those searing passages in Mississippi, in the autobiography, about Wright's library card? I read them first when I was fourteen years old.

Teaching makes you see the weak parts of yourself because you can't just skip over them. What I do on Saturday is harder than a full week at the university library. But I feel totally alive. It's one of the best things I ever did for myself.

It's a gray morning, and I wish you'd send me some of those arts and crafts you talk about. I'm writing this letter in the bathtub. I sprained my back.

Love,
Kate

5

Everybody left early, and nobody brought pot luck. Only four people came anyway. We drank whiskey out of water glasses, and radio reports on the riots replaced the Modern Jazz Quartet. We nibbled some moldy saltines and listened to noises from the alley. The city is burning and the delis and tailor shops along Dexter are gutted. It's the fourth night of the curfew. The 101st Airborne is quartered at Eastern High School across town. Here the National Guard is fat and disorganized, and they shoot each other. Today they buried a ten-year-old girl, and more rioting broke out. It's worse at four o'clock, and the newsboy doesn't deliver the paper anymore.

I wrapped up in my yellow quilt with the a/c on high. Parker called from Tel Aviv. She was crying. I considered my dead bolts and window bars and the spiked fence I added when I spruced up the place. I thought about the police and heat and Buddy's Barbecue. Twelfth Street is gone.

On Woodward Avenue, the Red Cross was collecting blood for riot victims, and they fed everybody orange juice and donuts and turned away the anemics. I was one of them. I walked over to the fire station with a plate of sandwiches and realized how foolish I was. Criminals loose on the sidewalk, not a woman in sight, or a cab. The fire captain put his hand on my shoulder, and I left.

I laid in a supply of gin and Maxwell House and pulled the shades. The sun still came in the high windows on each side of the fireplace, and dust settled in the air. Then I did the sensible thing. I copied my address book. The new one has two Chinese women on the cover. I copied it in one night because I couldn't sleep; then I rang up Herr Beil and told him I was scared to death, not of the riots, of my dreams. He came down in his robe, his cane nowhere in sight, and we ate breakfast at five A.M. in my kitchen. He brought bran muffins, frozen, and my teeth chattered. We talked about the nursery rhyme in *The Tin Drum:* "Witch, Witch, black as pitch . . ."

"A boogeyman," I said. "My boogeyman is worse than anything on these streets." My boogeyman keeps getting nearer, like death itself. The black cook in the German nursery rhyme turns blacker. What does that mean? There was a knock at the door, but we didn't answer it.

Herr Beil ate every crumb. I considered reading *The Tin Drum* in the original—another one of my pipe dreams. I know my limitations. The old requirement in German doesn't take me very far. Anyway, all I got was a "gentleman's C."

We washed the dishes together. He dried, and the soapy water felt good on my hands.

6

August 24, 1967

Dear Parker,

One of my students was killed in the riots. A short boy who carried a lead pipe the last Saturday I saw him. The funeral was over before I knew he was dead.

The damage here is in the black neighborhoods and to black people. Dexter is a mile farther up Grand Boulevard, but you can smell the smoke on my back porch.

The class met today. We're giving all our time to Baldwin's essays now: the ideas, the words, the honesty; *The Fire Next Time* is right here.

I don't feel easy with these five students, yet they come and they ask questions. The girl is subdued, but her journal isn't. Her brother was shot by a policeman a year ago. A case of mistaken identity. You don't want to know the details. She works in a furniture store that she says should have burned too. They sell on time and the furniture breaks down before the time runs out. Her sentence, not mine.

I sit at home Saturday afternoon and make plans for next Saturday. I wonder what I can say that matters. One student offered me a steak. He's a butcher's apprentice. The steak was "hot." "I'm no cook," I said. I dream about his blood-stained apron and the lead pipe.

At five o'clock I tried to write a sympathy card to the dead student's mother, but his death seems so awful and the card so perfunctory that I just sat still for awhile, and put it in the drawer. I'm going to bed early. It's been a long week.

Katie

◢7

Sept. 10, 1967

Dear Parker,

Dr. Koltonow is talking about the riots, about death, about Detroit. Over a year ago, the city was stunned by a murder in the suburbs. Dr. Koltonow raised his voice and turned red when he talked about it. A rabbi from Southfield was shot by a disturbed college student he had counseled. Right in the sanctuary. The student had one or two sessions with a psychiatrist. Then it happened.

"Nobody can predict the future, Miss McGhee."

Everybody looks for someone to pin it on. The student blamed the world on the wealthy congregation and picked the rabbi as a symbol. The librarians think the psychiatrist should have locked up the killer before he picked up the gun; and we have a few anti-Semites who keep their mouths shut and grin. Where is the villain? The world seems like a slaughterhouse these days.

I got a birth announcement from Harvey Sherman with a little note. It meant a lot to me. I'm sending him a stainless steel cup and plate from Denmark with a little elephant etched in the middle. They had a girl, Claudia, and they live right in Savannah. There's not much union work down there, so he joined his father's firm.

Are you serious about me coming to Israel? Your place, as you describe it, isn't big enough for the children, let alone me. But frankly I don't feel like going anywhere. I am brushing up on my German. I still have that picture of Marlene Dietrich that you liked. It's in the kitchen now.

I hired a caretaker Friday—free rent and my TV. There's a lot of room in the basement, and he gets it all with six cans of paint and a mattress. A student at Wayne. He has another job, too. I hope he stays. It's a relief to forget about lightbulbs and lawnmowers. He drives a motorcycle and keeps it in front of his bed.

Love,
Kate

P.S. I finally sent a letter to the dead student's mother. The new caretaker mailed it for me. Why would anyone want to predict the future?

Love again,
Kate

◢ 8

"I don't like boots." He said it in German: "Ich kann Stiefel nicht ausstehen."

It was Saturday afternoon and lunch was my idea. Herr Beil did not hesitate. We met at the front door. "How was your morning?" he added, presumably to dilute his opinion.

I tried to show off my lessons: "Es ist immer eine dankbarer Aufgabe."

"Eine *dankbare* Aufgabe, Kathrina."

It was a mistake in gender. We walked in the entryway and dumped our packages in the wing chair. He followed me into the kitchen and watched while I opened a can of soup and cut some bread. He was careful getting into a chair. First he hung his cane on the windowsill. My curtains are loaded with soot, and a few specks showed on the wooden handle.

Saturday afternoons are hard for me. I'm hyped from the students, and there's nobody to talk to after they go. Since the riots, walking makes it worse. The fires leveled too much.

Today, the students met me at the Detroit Institute of Arts and, coming up the steps, I had a spell of nostalgia. The arthritic woman behind the glass case in the gift shop is the same one who felt gossip was life when I worked here nine years ago. I steered everybody to the Rivera murals, and we talked about work. Mexican men and women, their squat bodies, the weight of their load, the very idea of art plastered in a wall, plenty to see, plenty to say. My stomach was upset, so I begged off on lunch.

Anyway, Herr Beil was an accidental pleasure. A breeze blew the curtains. A few leaves fell. I poured the wine and passed the salt. I watched him unfold his paper napkin. "Why don't you like them?" I said, looking at my new boots.

"They hide your ankles," he smiled, slowly removing his glasses. "Kathrina . . ."

I've worn boots with runover heels all my life. These were a hundred dollars, on sale. Flat heels. Brown leather. They almost touched my knees.

Boots. Other boots. On the pavement, in a city where streets aren't salted, and snow plows don't run. A city with more history than the automobile offers up. Berlin. How old was Herr Beil when Hitler came to power? How did boots sound, there, then?

"Oh, I suppose the salt will get to them in the end!" I wasn't thinking about the weather when I bought them.

Like wingtip shoes—dependable, powerful—like money in the bank, and one season following another. Boots for the future. And, if they hide my ankles, so much the better.

Space hung between our soup spoons. The faucet dripped. I dropped the pepper mill; and gradually our words picked up speed.

"My mother had a pepper-and-salt shaker that she put on the table for special occasions. The pepper was a tulip. The salt was a rose. Silver."

Herr Beil has a cross on his living room wall. A rosary on his pile of newspapers. Franz Kafka was a German Jew—from Prague. What did Herr Beil mean, destroyed? Sorrow is not destruction.

I took his hand. "Let's sit near my books." We walked slowly into the front room. I moved our packages out of the wing chair. He took the rocker. I wanted to say more. I wanted to do something. He kept his glasses on.

My stomach rumbled, and my feet hurt from the new leather. We continued talking around everything until I had to get up and go to the bathroom. Then he left. His cane hit the stairs with more force than I expected.

I feel asleep on the couch and dreamed about my great grandmother. This time Herr Beil took her hands away from my throat and held me close. My ankles were wet, and my blistered feet bare. "You don't need boots," he whispered, over and over. It's a dream I would like to have again.

I lay still and remembered Francis—his hands, his five o'clock shadow—and I felt what has happened to my breasts, in the years between.

October 1, 1967

Dear Kate,

Ben knew the rabbi and his wife, Goldie. He met them at some fundraiser when he was in engineering school. She gave her time and love to consoling the killer's mother. There was a feature on it in the *New York Times*.

What makes people really crazy? I worry about the girls. War is everywhere. I worry about everything. That rabbi was a wise man. He wrote books. He took risks. Now he's gone.

The girls love their overalls. We do a lot of climbing, and they do a lot of falling.

How about a trip to Greece next summer? We could rent a house. Burn your baggy dresses and buy a bathing suit. Olive trees and lemon orchards. Right up your alley, Kate. Let's do it.

Parker

◢ 10

October 18, 1967

Dear Parker,

I'm in a terrible rut. Buy my ticket with yours. I'll go. I cut off my hair, thinking the change would help. But this haircut is stylish and very expensive and has to be cut every three weeks. The reference librarian told me it needed hoop earrings. She thinks she is tactful.

I have no appetite for the right things; maybe Greek food . . . the wine tastes like eraser filings . . . maybe . . . the feta . . .

My German is coming along. Herr Beil and I have coffee after work on Fridays. He brings chocolate bars, and we skip supper and keep on with the lessons. We play German lieder and forget about the news. Did I tell you I gave my TV to the caretaker? Today we had charlotte russe with raspberry sauce. He told me I look like a cadaver, so I ate two pieces.

Bye,
Kate

◢ 11

October 25, 1967

Dear Parker,

The brightest boy in the group is a black separatist. His name is
Dudley. He should be in college. He avoids any word of why
he quit school or if he plans to go back. He talks about power:
politics, cars, money, dogs. . . . At first he wrote about his
philosophy as if it came from an outline; then he wrote some
of the whys and they were well thought out. His penmanship
wasn't odd in my grandmother's day—the backhand—but
now any handwriting so perfect, so bold, is the exception. He
follows directions like a robot. But he doesn't know what to
do with the admonition to write "anything" in the journal.
He obviously can't write "anything." So when I give samples, he
gives me a sample of each sample. Some personal, most
distanced. He's trying for balance; he's trying not to kick in
the wall, and he never misses a Saturday. I have to be careful that
these classes are not a dialogue between the two of us.

He is already near the end of his third steno pad. I collect
them every other Saturday and leave them with the branch
librarian Monday afternoon—with comments and suggestions
of things to read. I rarely touch the syntax, but he makes so
few mistakes that I correct them.

The class is taking a reading break. We went to the
Greyhound bus station last Saturday and sat for an hour, apart,
and then ate Chinese and talked about what we heard. We
talked about how people look when they don't talk and what
they do with their hands. "Isn't this spying?" the girl, Helen,
said. "Yes, but you are spying on yourself, too."

They pick out funny things, and I see the sad. The bus station
has almost everything—if you sit long enough. We even
eavesdropped while we ate. Two spoiled children were sitting
across from us—pouring soy sauce on the floor. A woman in
a navy suit sitting alone stared at us the whole time. We

were loud and kept interrupting each other and nobody wanted it to end.

Next week we decided to go to a different place (each of us) and meet at Grand Circus Park at noon to talk. Helen's mother is packing fried chicken, and Dudley is bringing Cokes. Someone is always absent or late, so we are only four, for the duration, it looks like. Nobody has quit yet. They just have other lives.

I have nobody now. I feel cold and heavy.

Kate

▲ 12

Nov. 10, 1967

Dear Parker,

Raymon Black came in the library today. He's looking for a tall teenager for a one-act play written by a local and directed by Tony Brown. I gave him Dudley's phone number, and we talked for a while on a bench in front of the library. He's full of stories that aren't so funny two hours later. Acting is his hobby.

He teaches special ed to delinquent boys on the East Side. He can't use his sick time because substitutes won't go there. The regular teachers have to double up classes when a teacher is out. Sounds impossible. He has taught *Hamlet*. Not the usual way. He has eight boys (three can't read) and he never turns his back. "It's not a job for an old man," he says. He wanted to be a high school history teacher, but white men are in line, knee deep, for that one. He didn't need to tell me, and he didn't.

His funniest story was about his son, who whispered to his fourth-grade teacher that his mother sucked blood and his daddy wore a big black cape and went out every night, late. The school psychologist called them both in. His wife is a lab tech, and he was rehearsing *Dracula* over at U. of D.

"You've got to do something physical," Dr. Koltonow says. I feel rotten, but he says I'm getting well.

Do you have any ideas? For the time being, I'm sanding an oak rocker I bought for ten dollars at a junk shop. I've got papers spread all over the kitchen floor, and I moved the coffee pot and oranges into the living room. "Does this suit you?" I asked Dr. Koltonow. "Sand a little harder, Miss McGhee." He was serious. I hate to say this, but it helps my insomnia. I also bought a jump rope, my idea, and I can be found skipping around with nothing on but my bra at six A.M. The imagery is ridiculous. The caretaker asked me what I was

140

doing. He is up early studying, and the noise had him wondering.

Love,
Kate

▲ 13

Dear Parker,
The class is writing about their childhoods and/or money. I figure a choice is always good.

I got home before a thunderstorm rocked a few things loose outside and then I sat down at my desk. You remember the one Francis had at the bookstore? I was considering refinishing it but stopped in time. I followed my own directions (with the writing, not the desk) and came up with these episodes. I kept crossing out and starting over, and, in the end, more paper was on the floor than on the table, and the sun had come out.

Let's call it an early start on my memoirs. What do you think, Parker? Is it schmaltz?

Love,
Kate

P.S. I could use a letter from you at this point.

Enclosures/2

Childhood

My mother gave me oblique directions on my fate as a woman. She alerted me to germs and physical danger, and invariably these enemies were found in large families whose numbers alone made supervision impossible, where doors were left open, mayonnaise jars waited uncovered on the kitchen table. . . . "The mother's fault for having so many kids. How can money be spread that thin?" She pointed out these lessons when a girl got pregnant, when a boy quit school or ran away, or when a passerby's winter coat did not meet her standards for warmth. My mother guessed the cause of polio before Salk, and she never let me near a swimming pool. I learned to slice potatoes when I was twelve. Knives worried her, too.

There was one occasion when she was speechless—when the lesson was too perfect, the imagery too vivid, the punishment too great, even for her.

A woman with five children lived directly across the street from us. I could see the pattern in the lace curtains on their bay window from my couch. Once, the oldest daughter knocked at our front door to borrow an egg. Her drawstring skirt, made from a feedsack, did not protect her from the rain. My mother made her wait outside. "They have bedbugs," she warned.

The day it happened, I don't remember waking up, just looking out the window.

The sky is on fire. The whole house disappeared behind orange flames. All I see is my mother's pink chenille bathrobe. She is leaning against the spare tire on the Hupmobile. Axes, hoses are in somebody's hands, but no ambulance comes. My mother and three firemen walk back and forth; they carry the small bodies to her car.

Neighbors rush in and pull the blankets from my bed to wrap the bodies in. My mother squeezes behind the steering wheel, and the car moves forward. There are no sounds in this memory.

My mother drove the children to the hospital. Three died on the way, and the fourth lived a few hours.

We had no phone, so that night Joe Green came over to tell us the fire started before dawn when the oldest girl tried to light the oil stove. Her mother had been sick a long time, and the smallest children slept in her bed to keep her warm. The bedroom had no window and when the firemen chopped through the wall they assumed the stove had blown up because the oldest girl's corpse was missing an arm.

Some thought my mother's neighborliness was valiant, but I saw it for what it was, and I didn't learn not to play with matches, or to always check a diaphragm for holes before inserting it. I didn't come away from those horror-filled moments with the knowledge that ignorance and poverty court disaster. What I saw, instead, was a mother who loved her children more than my mother ever could. A woman who would have died of pneumonia, if the stove had not exploded, with her arms above her head and sweat soaking the cold sheets. And I drew one other moral: Wasn't I left alone all day, every day, next to an oil stove with kitchen matches on a shelf above my head? Any lesson my mother wanted to teach had to include those facts, and we both knew it.

Money

In the neighborhood where I grew up, money meant a lot. Two girls I knew undressed in front of a third girl's grandfather who paid the group five dollars to see and touch a little. He kept his pants on and smoked a cigar. Sometimes, too, he took his granddaughter and a few friends for rides in his Model T. They came back with big banana splits in plastic containers and ate them sitting in the freshly cut grass while the old man watched the frayed edges of their shorts.

When seeds were sold by the Girl Scouts in the spring, most people didn't answer the door. Some fathers bought one or two packages of vegetables, but the live-in grandfather was a soft touch we all knew could be ours. We were tempted.

Our fathers, too, felt the pull of the forbidden. The local barber doubled as a bookie. A running crap game hit the alleys in back of the small shops in the neighborhood every summer afternoon. Few Fridays passed without a poker game on somebody's back porch. A friendly game, in the beginning, but men had been known to wager their hunting rifles in the hours after midnight.

If our mothers were tempted, it was their secret. They stood like a Greek chorus—proponents of thrift, suspicious of danger—easier to spot in a bookie than a kindly grandfather.

▲14

December 26, 1967

Parker,

I'm tempted to paint this blasted rocking chair. I made a list
for the hardware store and tore it up. Home improvement
is not for me. How can anyone waste time on such mindless
activity? I should have paid to have it stripped.

It's hard to believe Christmas has come and gone. I had a little
party. Herr Beil and my old French instructor from L'Alsace.
You remember the one with the pointer and wooden leg
who scared me half to death? And the newest clerk at the
library. She's a lit major from Hamtramck. I told everybody to
bring along whomever they liked, and we'd trim the tree.
I bought a blue spruce and lit the fire. We still drink Cutty
Sark around here, and after the riots, I make sure I don't run out.

The French instructor brought his wife and the clerk brought
her half-brother. Everyone brought an ornament, and they
stayed all night. Around midnight Herr Beil fell asleep in
the wing chair, and we left him alone.

The clerk's brother sat a fifth of Old Bushmill's on the
kitchen table and picked up a teacup. He must be used to ethnic
jokes with a background like his. He slips into a brogue
when he has enough whiskey. It turned out to be a room full
of fallen-away Catholics. We sang carols, and I fiddled with a
red velvet dove while everyone else put tinsel on the tree.

How can I describe it—like a cloud being lifted—choose
your own cliché!

The fire smelled sweet, and I felt safe in my new clothes.
A kimono with a high neck—black. The Irishman threw some
tinsel in my hair when he took his sister home. My French
instructor mumbled something about New Year's Eve and
saw to it that Herr Beil made it to the top of the stairs. I went
to bed and slept the whole day. At five I got up and washed
the plates and glasses and made myself an eggnog. Somebody

spilled nutmeg on the floor, and I left it there. The phone rang and it was the Irishman. He asked me how I felt about plum pudding.

"I like it," I said.

"How about having some for breakfast? I'll bring it over."

"Call me in the morning," I said, and crashed down the receiver. I'm in no mood for a smooth operator.

You won't believe this, but the next morning, he called at eight and invited me out for eggs. The menu changes with the response. It's called jockeying for position. He scares me. The first thing he asked was why I lived in this building. "Because I own it," I smiled. So far he hasn't kissed me, but he has bed on his mind. And I have a week off on mine . . . are you laughing? I am.

Love and kisses,
Kate

◢15

December 30, 1967

Dear Parker,
The Irishman from Hamtramck is putting up a subdivision
not far from Cranbrook. It's a life of slide rules and sawdust,
and thank God he doesn't talk about it. He wears khaki pants
and a white shirt and work boots and a plaid jacket. He lives
with his mother and sister and drives a new truck. His old one
was smashed by some goons from the union. TEAMSTERS.
I'm afraid to ask what he reads because it's likely to be
Field and Stream. We are going tobogganing in Rouge Park
tonight and to that party on New Year's Eve.
Love,
Kate

◢ 16

We're off to a hot start with my legs around him, down the hill, and just short of the evergreens. The lights are bright on the snow. Rouge Park is a wholesome menace. Worse than skiing!

"Kate, have you lived in this house long?" We are back in my kitchen deciding between hot cocoa and calvados.

"Two years."

"It's not the safest place."

"I'm not looking for safety. It's a mile from my job and across the street from the bank." The best defense is at hand: "I guess you took your childhood seriously," I add. "The building blocks . . . the erector sets . . . those little saws?"

Snow melts off his boots on the hardwood floor. I get up and bend over a basket of logs. He walks behind me and puts both hands around my waist. I guess you'd call it a hug. He's strong. Neither of us moves for a minute. "Do you want to build the fire?" I say. "I'm a little weak in the knees." After I'm settled in the wing chair, he drops a log on his foot and rips up the evening paper. "The kindling is in the corner," I point out the obvious.

Calvados sears off the blood vessels in my mouth. His hands are under my sweater. My breasts are my strongest asset, if you're traveling that road. I know it, and he knows it. I end up bent over the footstool with his hands where I like them. Fortunately, the caretaker went home for Christmas, and Herr Beil is almost deaf.

January 16, 1968

Dear Parker,

Have taken up in earnest with the Irishman from Hamtramck.
We tried ice skating after tobogganing and then we went to
bed. New Year's Eve is a blur. We were invited to a party,
but I sent flowers instead—the last Christmas cactus at the
florist.

Do you remember "A Child's Christmas in Wales"? You
gave me the record. As close to Irish as I could get. We played it
over and over. We drank eggnog for breakfast and supper,
and he invited me to go deer hunting in the Upper Peninsula.
The two of us. Do I need to tell you what I said? He went
anyway, with his family, and came back with a venison roast
which he insisted I cook. It tasted like tallow.

Today he arrived with a sack of potatoes and a gallon of
Old Bushmill's and told me I'd have to buy a green sweater
or the affair was off. A joke, of sorts. I took off to the army
surplus and came back with an olive drab flyer's sweater.
You know the kind of leather shoulders and three buttons up the
front? You can go through the motions and still be yourself!

A meat and potatoes man. He helped me finish up the rocker,
and we went out together to get a cushion for it. It's been
snowing all week. It's snowing now and rain is predicted.

Is it too soon to say he is close to his mother and she won't like
you or Ben, for that matter? I'm not getting into it on paper,
but a few details tell the story. She fancies she knows me
because she knows where I work and where I live and how old I
am. And she is half right! She wants her son to marry a girl
five years younger, not five years older.

In spite of everything, I'm trying to relax and enjoy this. I'm
concentrating on what I can see and touch. I'm sleeping all
night. And my appointments are down to two a month.

But the best news is quite simple. I haven't forsaken my

German lessons or the Sunday night suppers or tried to fit them into this romance. And I refuse Sunday dinners with the family. Life isn't a jigsaw puzzle. It shouldn't have to be a series of compartments, either; but that's all I can manage, and I'll take it.

My hair is growing out. Blondes turn a dirty gray, but it doesn't seem to matter.

My Christmas cards were the usual UNICEFs, except for one. A big poinsettia on parchment with one gold ball hanging from a leaf. Harvey's way of telling me he got a divorce and will be doing some consulting work with the UAW this spring. I wrote him a note on my new stationery and asked him if he had lost his taste for martinis. I also sent Claudia *Where the Wild Things Are.* I got a letter in the return mail with a crystal pitcher. I went right out and bought a jar of big olives. I hate lemon twists and all that goes with them. What do you think, Parker? Have I become a practical woman or a fool?

Love,
Kate

◢18

I am sitting in a straight-backed chair Dr. Koltonow must have picked up at a junk shop too. It's a cloudy afternoon. My last appointment.

"Just remember, Miss McGhee, you'll never be happy being Mrs. Sally Smith!"

"What kind of remark is that?"

He smiles and shakes my hand. We are standing at the side of his Eames chair. The footstool is being recovered. Even leather must be kept up. Is this all? No quotes from Freud? No summary? No clichés?

Last night I dreamed about him. He's only eleven years older and already gray. There's a little scar above his right eye from a car wreck last year. But it's his words, written on banners, in fragments, without benefit of an ellipsis, that flashed through my sleeping mind, and somehow these words mean more than any stripped-down rocker or new lover with work boots and a bigoted soul. Hard words. Simple words. Proverbs, too.

Outside it is pouring, but who cares about the rain? Or the gray slush? Weather isn't the source of anybody's depression. There's a Russian proverb about beets and potatoes and shit and farmers and the weather, but I'm crying so hard the stanza won't come together. I'm crying because I'm happy inside. Because my clothes are plastered to my body, and, for once, it doesn't bother me one bit!